Praise fo

'Eclectic, accomplish
literature in discove
in all sorts of directions, yet remains centred around
one consistent premise: the joy of the written word.'

Kit Caless

'An amazingly diverse list. All the stories have their own
unique energy, originality and power.'

Zoe Gilbert

'Arrives and lands with thrilling confidence, quickly
establishing an atmosphere that is subtle but indelible.'

Emma Paterson, on the 2019 winner

'I was about to submit a story for the Brick Lane Bookshop's
Short Story Prize when I thought, "Hmm, I should probably
read the stuff they usually pick first." Well, the calibre is
damn high. And it's such a pleasure reading new voices – I
can't wait to read more from each author featured on the
longlist.'

Megan Thomas, Goodreads

'One of the best multi-author short-story collections that
I have read in recent years. The 2019 longlist achieved an
impressive feat, demonstrating the variety and power of the
form.'

Jarred McGinnis

Brick Lane Bookshop
Short Story Prize

Longlist 2020

A Brick Lane Bookshop Publication

Designed, typeset and project-managed by Kate Ellis

First published by Brick Lane Bookshop in 2020

ISBN 978-1-91620-821-6

Brick Lane Bookshop
166 Brick Lane
London
E1 6RU

www.bricklanebookshop.org

A CIP record for this book is available from the British Library

Printed and bound in Great Britain by Clays Ltd, Elcograf S.p.A.

To all the writers who entered this year's
competition, despite everything.

Contents

Foreword

Denise Jones

Forty years ago there were no bookshops in Tower Hamlets. When one of the largest high-street bookstores was asked why, their reply was that people in the East End didn't read! Not so. From the early seventies I was involved with a thriving community arts scene in London's East End. There were projects with local residents in writing, drama, film and video, photography, music, dance, visual arts, murals and festivals. Centerprise Bookshop in Hackney, Basement Writers in Cable Street, and Stepney Books, set up by Celia Stubbs, Jenny Smith, Jo Chesterton and me in Tower Hamlets, east London, were publishing poetry, local history and autobiographies, and running busy reading groups and writers' workshops. But the area still lacked a good general bookshop.

In 1978 an opportunity arose from a year-long community arts festival, Tower Hamlets Arts Project (THAP), to open a community bookshop called THAP Books. A group of us leased an empty mini-supermarket in Whitechapel and set up a charity, THAP, with the bookshop as the not-for-profit trading arm. Supported by the Arts Council (through the Greater London Arts Association (GLAA)), the writers' workshops, publishing ventures, author signings and schools' bookstalls grew in popularity and we changed the name to Eastside Books / Eastside Arts Wordcentre. To offer people from Tower Hamlets, Newham and Hackney the chance to be published we ran the Eastside Stories Novel Bursary competition from 1994–98, with a sponsored cash prize and an introduction to a leading literary agent for the winner.

When Eastside Arts Wordcentre closed in 2004 I moved the bookshop to Brick Lane.

Fast-forward fourteen years and two desires converged: I had the idea to refresh the Eastside Stories Novel Bursary, while Kate Ellis had been fostering a dream to run a short story competition. I wanted to sponsor an initiative that gave aspiring writers an opportunity to be published; Kate, one of our bookshop team and an emerging writer herself, was interested in taking the idea forward on behalf of Brick Lane Bookshop.

The outcome, in 2019, was the inaugural Brick Lane Bookshop Short Story Competition, established with a first prize of £1,000 and the same ethos as the bookshop, which is to create opportunities that allow people to take on new challenges and acquire new skills.

I'm very grateful to last year's readers, who selected a longlist of twelve stories from 463 entries, and to the judges, Emma Paterson, Kit Caless and Zoe Gilbert, who chose the shortlist and the winners, and am extremely proud of the resulting publication: *Brick Lane Bookshop Short Story Prize: Longlist 2019*.

In 2020, we are delighted that Harriet Moore, Sharmaine Lovegrove and Chris Power agreed to be judges and have chosen the shortlist and prizewinners. My thanks also go to the amazing Brick Lane Bookshop team and the twenty-one readers who between them sifted through 1,134 stories to create the longlist. Be assured that submissions to the competition are completely anonymised before they are read.

We expected some stories to be first tries and some to be from more experienced writers. Historically, the mainstream publishing industry hasn't been structured around the nurturing of emerging talent, though more recently, small presses are publishing new and diverse voices. In order for new writers who are not on publishers' lists to be heard, there must be opportunities in the public arena for open discussion and criticism. There are numerous competitions and writing courses but few publications of the entries or output, so I hope our competition and anthology introduce some exciting new writers and will help them to become better known.

The launch events of these books of short stories are important social celebrations. They're occasions for bringing together all the people who contributed to and helped create the book: writers, readers, production team and printers; other writers, friends, families and neighbours. The readings from the stories are the highlights and this year we'll make sure we meet and congratulate the amazing winners on the internet if we're unable to get together in person because of the pandemic.

Finally, many congratulations to this year's winner, Alice Haworth-Booth, for her story 'The Closed Door'.

I'm delighted that the number of entries for 2020's competition almost tripled and am looking forward to

reading even more submissions to the Brick Lane Bookshop
Short Story Competition in 2021.

Denise Jones
August 2020

Introduction
Kate Ellis

I went to the supermarket today and the woman on the till asked how I was, looking over my mask to my eyes as she spoke, as though she wanted a real answer. I've noticed in the bookshop, too, since we've reopened, customers are expressing concern; they're happy the shop is still here and seem to enjoy talking to people not in their household. These micro interactions have accrued new value. We didn't know we'd miss them. They used to be throwaway, like a lot of things: looking into the distance, leaving the country, wandering into shops, pubs or restaurants with our faces showing.

Walking to work again, I've been relieved to see strangers I used to pass almost every day. The ginger guy who cycles with his head down is still pedalling, the man outside the bagel shops is still sitting, the woman on the till at Tesco is doing OK. She's wondering what the hurry is to return to normal; she doesn't know why people are rushing, because life goes on, doesn't it?

I was happy that the Short Story Prize could go on this year. When London was silenced and the bookshop closed in March, being able to run the prize gave me structure, and felt like a real privilege. At a time when we could see almost no one unless they were pixelated, reading the stories provided necessary glimpses into the minds of others.

I'm grateful to Brick Lane Bookshop, as ever, for funding the prize, and also to every writer who, in the strangest of circumstances, had the focus and discipline to produce and submit a story. It's heartening to know that so many people, between feeding themselves and washing up on repeat, looking after their work, dependants and mental states all under the same roof, decided to spend their spare time writing, editing and submitting a short story. The response was humbling and impressive. Zadie Smith writes in *Intimations*, 'I do feel comforted to discover I'm not the only person on this earth who has no idea what life is for, nor what is to be done with all this time aside from filling it.' Writing is as good a way as any; it gives us 'something to do'.

It felt as though many of the entries were outlets for characters and writers alike. Many wanted to escape or had done so; there were literal and non-literal lockdowns. Quite a few considered harsh external realities and fragile interior lives.

Our 2020 judging panel were Sharmaine Lovegrove, of the ever-ascending Dialogue Books, Harriet Moore of David Higham Associates literary agency, and Chris Power, author of *Mothers* and of the *Guardian*'s *A brief survey of the short story*. We're extraordinarily lucky to have all of them on board.

The Zoom meeting to discuss and decide the shortlist and winners was fascinating and passionate. Between inevitable interferences from cats' bottoms, excitable dogs and children's missing teeth, the words 'profound', 'moving', 'funny' and 'polished' were used to describe the longlist.

We debunked the persistent myth that short stories are easier to consume than novels. Flannery O'Connor says: 'A good short story should not have less meaning than a novel, nor should its action be less complete.' As such, stories are not easily dipped in and out of. They require concentration, focus, and mental agility. They are not novel-length comforting hugs; they're spiky, challenging and mind-bending, but maybe that's why I love them.

Perhaps more than ever, we as readers were drawn to stories that took us elsewhere. The longlist transports us to Kerala, Italy, Scotland, coastal England, Chicago, Tanzania, Syria, and of course, London. Subjects covered include dystopian raves, climate change, love, austerity, addiction, micro aggressions, hope, dyed kittens, grief, homophobia, shed-dwelling, hip-hop, acid attacks, fraying marriage, clam pasta, and mental health. After almost two hours' discussion, 'The Closed Door' was agreed upon as a winner for its light touch, humour, seriousness, and original voice.

We had 1,134 entries to the competition, which far exceeded our wildest expectations. We're enormously grateful to so many people for choosing to support the shop and the prize.

The aim of the Short Story Prize is to find new, exciting and diverse voices, to reward and publish outstanding stories, and to connect their authors with readers and audiences they haven't encountered before.

We've almost sold out of our inaugural anthology.

Alongside selling it in our shop and at other, brilliant independents, we've posted it to customers as far away as Honolulu, Copenhagen and Edinburgh – it's travelled more than any of us this year and I hope the 2020 issue goes even further. I hope, too, that you enjoy the stories in this book and that they transport you, whether you can currently leave the house or not.

Another bookshop straying into publishing is No Alibis in Belfast. In the introduction to their recent anthology *Still Worlds Turning*, June Caldwell writes: 'There really is no covert set of rules. All you can do is keep reading and writing short stories, savouring, quarrelling with, trying to understand them.' I intend to.

Kate Ellis
August 2020

Brick Lane Bookshop
Short Story Prize
Longlist 2020

The Closed Door
Alice Haworth-Booth

The baby was going through a phase of only saying Hello,
though it knew a lot of other words. Hello! it said to Rona
when she came home. Then Hello! when Rona gave it a
yogurt, and Hello! when Rona put it to bed. It was nice to be
greeted but Rona wondered where Cat and Dog and No had
gone. She wasn't even Rona's baby but of course Rona had
a certain investment in her. The baby wasn't sleeping well;
the nights were too hot. Her face with its glaze of distraught
boredom, paralysed on the verge of tears in the cot, was too
much sometimes. Rona had gone back to bed to listen to
waves crashing through her earphones.

The baby, if it belonged to anyone, was her boyfriend
Joe's. He'd had her by accident with a short-lived sweetheart
named Dawn. In the delivery room they had named the baby
Brenda, making her seem, Rona had always thought, more
like a colleague or an aunt than a baby. For Rona, having
this kind of baby solved a lot of problems. She could see
how she liked it and leave at any time. She could choose to
cancel plans with the baby if something else came up. Joe
was grateful if she helped even half-heartedly.

They had met when Rona was handing out flyers for a protest.

1

In a way, Joe had been her only real political success. There was something about flyering that emboldened Rona: instead of hating her, people on the street hated something much bigger. They hate life itself! she told herself. 'Piss off,' a man with a wheelie suitcase had volleyed at her as she smiled and shouted, 'Save the world! Next Saturday!' A woman had taken a flyer and started reading it before asking if Rona had any facts, and Rona, caught off guard, had replied that she didn't have a mind for facts. The woman was shaking her head.

'If I were you I'd *get* a mind for facts,' the woman said, 'if you're going to go around asking people to sign up for this drivel.'

She'd walked away, looking back at Rona at intervals shouting, 'Educate yourself!'

Rona did know a few facts, but she was philosophically resistant to repeating them. Either you could imagine the apocalypse or you couldn't. She didn't want to convince anyone else the world was going to end. It felt cruel. Rona preferred to smile at people without saying anything.

Other passers-by had been nice. A dental student who had been at Tahrir Square complimented Rona on her government: 'You have a wonderful country – don't try to change it too much. Just a couple of tweaks, OK?' Rona nodded and wished him luck in his orthodontic exams. She felt good again; this was good, people were real, they were all fighting their own battles.

A man in a blue shirt had come over to her and asked for a leaflet, though she was already holding one out to him.

'Hello,' she said, when he didn't walk away.

He said he didn't agree with their methods, though it was

true something needed to be done. Rona's group were known for irritating people. She wasn't sure if she agreed with their methods either, but their methods were really the main thing about them.

'I don't like conflict,' she'd said. 'Actually, I don't really like doing anything.'

'We're alike, then,' he said. 'I work there,' he added, gesturing to a government building Rona couldn't name.

'Right, I hear they hate doing things in there,' she said. Though most people wouldn't call it a dictatorship, the government was still no good, as far as she knew.

'I shouldn't even really be talking to you like this,' he said. 'I'll get in trouble.'

'Can they see us from up there?' Rona said. 'We could pretend to be having an argument.'

The man started to jab his finger at her, knitting his eyebrows together, looking as if he might say something like, 'Now listen here.'

'But anyway. It's good that you've thought so carefully about the inconvenience that you're causing. That's reassuring.'

'I frequently think about it,' Rona said.

The man pointed to the flyer. Whose Future? **OUR FUTURE!** it said, answering itself in bold, in capitals. 'It's a little possessive, isn't it? Who are "we"?'

'I didn't write the flyer,' Rona said. 'It's got nothing to do with me.'

When he left he said, 'Well, keep up the good work, but, you know, not really.'

Joe's baby must have already existed then, in a controversially embryonic, cellular, sloppy way. Rona was oddly stirred by thinking of Brenda's conception, her formation by the meeting of what she imagined were two steaming-hot substances – Rona had always had a loose grip on the science. She thought of it as cosmology: things happening in strange dimensions, at unfamiliar scales. Brenda was so small then, but Rona imagined planetary gases melding and churning.

Having a baby by accident was wildly out of Rona's character, which is probably why it hadn't happened to her. Her womb was resolutely closed. She knew you shouldn't think this way, but she felt familiar by now with the kind of person her reproductive system was. A strait-laced jobsworth, a woman in a pleated skirt, named . . . something like Brenda. It worked against desire; it put its calling on hold. Joe was obviously, somehow, pro-life, not in the political sense but optimistically, lustily in favour of it all.

She had next seen Joe at the protest she'd given him the flyer for.

'I'm not staying,' he'd said, when he found her with a bucket, shouting, 'Donations!' into the wind.

'No one's staying,' said Rona, feeling light-headed and hungry. 'The world is literally ending.' She laughed. 'Imagine if it was ending right now,' she said, striking a runner's pose, making as if to dash for it. Would it be like that?

'Aargh,' Joe cried, shielding his face against his destiny. 'Help!'

Rona shrugged. They stood for a moment, looking at placards.

'Anyway, thanks,' he said, and disappeared again without telling her his name or anything else about himself. He was wearing Nikes. Time felt short to Rona. She didn't have any to waste, but it also felt like a silky nothingness, whipping around above her head mockingly. It wasn't the tick-tock, sun-up-sun-down, winter-spring-summer-autumn, birth-middle-age-death time she'd grown up knowing. It was new, urgent and meaningless.

Joe started coming to meetings in community centres and in the tea-stained attics of obscure trade union buildings.

'Hey! You! Government mole! State-funded spy!' Rona yelled when she saw him, and people spun round to look, but he stayed while they discussed recycled sticker suppliers.

'I'm Joe,' he said.

Their fingers touched while putting the mugs away – the mugs all featured the faces and slogans of unsuccessful candidates and forgotten campaigns. Rona was comforted by them. She wanted to produce things that would become dusty, redundant and inexplicable. What did Choose Queues mean? To work away patiently at the margins of things, neatening them like a pastry crust. To contribute to life without being at its centre. Revolution is not a piece of embroidery, said Mao, who was wrong about so many things.

'Don't you find these mugs depressing?' Joe asked.

Rona shook her head. She wasn't sure she should say out loud that she was reassured by years of political failure. Joe was into progress, the irresistible thrum of it. Rona wouldn't mind if time stopped and pooled in on itself, making a large grey puddle.

'I'm just saying I would never want to end up on a mug,' he said.

Rona went to the toilet, locked the door and couldn't unlock it again. She pawed at the silver bolt for minutes, growing hot with embarrassment. Finally she saw Joe's shoes under the door, pacing for a moment before stopping, squishing under his weight as he crouched. His voice was saying, 'Rona? Rona, is that you?'

Rona had tears in her eyelashes by then. How can we go into the future with our noses pressed against a closed door? Is that what Virginia Woolf had said?

'Are you upset?'

'What?' Rona said.

'This is going to work,' he said. 'It won't be a mug.'

'A what?'

'A mug.'

Rona was thinking about Joe's face, imagining its concreteness. Was he talking about the revolution, or something more important?

'I'm not upset,' Rona said, weeping. 'I'm trapped.'

'Take a deep breath,' Joe said. 'Count to . . . six. After that, try the lock again?'

Rona didn't like to take a deep breath, but she wiped her eyes and looked up. There was a sign on the door that read: To unlock, pull towards you. Rona pulled the door and the bolt sprung back. Belief! It could be administered like WD40.

At the next meeting Joe was wirier, more glistening than usual, smelling of mineral water. Rona was kind of high, psychologically speaking. One of the leaders (there were no leaders) had asked her to be part of a secret cell. She couldn't tell Rona the details but it was high profile, very risky, very exciting. Rona had quickly said OK, though now she was thinking about it it seemed like a wild thing to do, whatever 'it' was going to be. She clutched Joe's shoulder, said 'Hi!' too charismatically.

'Guess what,' Joe said uncertainly when they'd sat down and people were still talking around them and making their tea. 'I'm having a baby.'

'Haha,' he added.

Rona nodded, thinking about all the things it could be, how they would get away, *whether* they'd get away. Would they have to get a taxi? They would have to lie about getting the taxi afterwards and say they rode their bikes.

'I'm sorry,' Joe was saying. 'I don't know if it's weird for you. I mean, it's obviously weirder for me. Maybe.'

'Sorry,' Rona said, 'what?'

In Any Other Business a drama teacher in orange leggings was suggesting they all lie down on their backs for fifteen minutes in town centres up and down the country, flailing their arms and legs. It's called the Dying Fly, she explained. There was some disagreement.

'I think it might be considered offensive,' said a soft-looking man.

'We'll look silly. Vulnerable. Like dying flies,' said another.

The drama teacher nodded.

Rona looked at Joe, who was contemplating the Dying Fly placidly.

'We would, of course, imbue it with pathos,' the woman said, finally.

Rona put her hand up, voting in favour of the Dying Fly. She wanted to lie down. She wanted to flail miserably. She wanted to die.

*

The end of the world sometimes seemed like a frivolous thing to get upset about, an existential crisis of last resort. There was going to be a sombre procession – mothers and children would dance sadly through the streets. 'Throwing another funeral for yourselves?' said a different man with a wheelie suitcase as Rona handed him the flyer.

Joe's baby was the size of an aubergine by now. *Your baby is the size of an eggplant, and can blink and dream*, Rona read online, Googling '28 weeks'. It was depressing looking at the cut-out photo of the aubergine, so large and real. *Your baby has a strong chance of survival if born now!* the website congratulated. Joe went on the march or mothers and children. Rona had gone too, though when she got there she looked out for the papier mâché skeletons and skulked along behind them. Skin in the game, the mothers were saying. 'What I'd really like,' said a small child into a microphone, 'is to live to the end of my natural life.'

She was sad, but what about? What was the end of the world anyway? Was it a substance like a gas that they were all walking through at all times, getting on their skins, making them feel grubby and itchy?

'Stupid time to have a baby,' Joe said when he found her.

'Ah, someone didn't do their research,' Rona said. Still, it wasn't imaginative to assume the worst. Got to enjoy it while it lasts. 'How about a drink?' she asked. It started raining hard.

They both ordered tap water at the pub, which was full of mothers and placards and prams. Rona kept bumping into children eating tin-foiled sandwiches on the way up the stairs.

They drank their water quickly and Joe went to get more.

While he was gone Rona listened to two friends talking about open borders. Joe came back with two glasses of water each.

'What's happening with your baby?' Rona ventured. 'Is it quite big by now?'

'I don't know,' said Joe. 'I don't get to see it much. You know, the bump. *In embryo*. I'm not with . . . It was very . . .' He trailed off and smiled downwards.

When they left the pub it had turned into a scorching evening. She could feel the heat pumping off the brick walls all the way back to Joe's house. 'Climate change in a day,' Rona said, to say something.

'Kind of a relief,' Joe replied. 'It would be better if we could just get it over with.'

He lived in a nice place with two other well-paid men. The walls were all subtle greys, the carpets were seagrass; the kitchen had a wooden counter smudged gently with olive-oil stains.

'I love you,' Joe said as they ate spaghetti in the dining area of the eat-in kitchen. His housemate was cooking behind them with his headphones on.

'Did you mean to say that?' asked Rona.

'I think so. What did I say?'

'"I love you."'

'Really?' Joe said.

Joe was trying to save the world; everyone was now. Joe's job title actually was Environmental, and Rona forgot the end. Officer. Liaison. Lead. Joe truly did do things every day. He made a difference. There were statistics that he was directly responsible for. Rona Googled it. Eighty-nine per cent decrease in this, 154% increase in that. Joe didn't tell her about it.

Then Joe's department put out a report Rona couldn't even look at the title of, and she didn't know how he could copy and paste it into spreadsheets and emails without shivering, but he always seemed pleased about something, and sent her texts that said things like 'Are you happy with linguine?'

Two months later Brenda was born. Brenda means Queen of the Land, Dawn told her when she went to the hospital. When Rona looked it up on her phone she found out Brenda meant sword. Brenda was a person, it was true, detached from Dawn and Joe, more Rona's, she felt, as she sat in the visitor's chair holding her. With Brenda in her arms Rona felt a dizzying love for the future, but when she handed her back to Dawn, it was gone again.

In the hospital Joe looked at Brenda like someone he truly loved. His eyes became browner, his eyebrows wriggled with a high-frequency pleasure that seemed both transmitted and received. Rona had never seen anything like it.

Now they were here in Joe's flat, the three of them and Brenda's chosen family of stuffed animals. This kind of motherhood required nothing. It was shockingly easy to make a life. Rona bought large pots of geraniums and put them on the windowsill. She ate two hours before yoga; she finally owned a camisole. Joe was here too, of course, though his life seemed mysterious and separate. Watering plants by a special method Rona didn't know the details of, over the sink. Sterilising things. Cutting slices of bread precisely, to

Brenda's exact requirements. He put up shelves and laid a blue fluffy carpet in Brenda's bedroom. He's handy! said Rona's friends winkingly.

Rona had a small worry that she and Joe would break up at a bad time developmentally. Would Brenda carry with her the vague, disturbing memory of a non-committal woman? Or remember nothing of Rona at all?

'Just when I've made a life, life on earth ends,' Rona said to Brenda as she chopped up a banana.

'What do you mean by "life"?' Joe asked.

'What do I mean by "ends"?' Rona replied.

Rona wondered if Brenda already knew about the end of the world in her wise, large-eyed way. Children were smarter than anyone, and more brave, though it was an irony that they did lack certain capabilities, that their access to power was indirect. The youngest of all of them, she was the closest in a way to not existing. It was very recently that she had not existed, within living memory you might say.

'Is existing better?' Rona asked Brenda, putting the banana down in front of her.

Joe was printing a report and the words 'doomsday clock' were coming out of the printer.

'Do you think Brenda will print things out?' Joe turned to Rona and asked. 'Do you think Brenda will know that jagged sound of cartridge on A4? Do you think Brenda will queue in shops and not know where to look as she taps her card to the card reader?'

'Brenda will place her items in the bagging area,' said Rona.

'Do you think Brenda will put elasticated blue plastic bags around her shoes when she goes swimming?'

11

'Do you think Brenda will have a terrible moth problem, will spend thousands of pounds trying to kill moths?'

'Do you think Brenda will desire nothing more than a pink pencil sharpener from the Natural History Museum?' Joe tapped Brenda on the head.

'OK,' said Rona.

In the bed which they have made an ocean, with the sea sounds on a speaker now, Rona wonders what constitutes a raft, whether two human bodies are enough.

'What will happen to Brenda?' Rona asks.

'Let's hope Brenda's life is strange,' says Joe.

A column of light appears at the sea's furthest shore, then broadens into a lighthouse beam. Brenda in her striped pyjamas climbs aboard. 'Hello,' she says.

'She's here,' Rona says.

'The future,' Joe says.

To Those Born Later
Kieran Toms

There is a valley, in Scotland, where the vineyards are now, and about a quarter of the way up one of the looming slopes there's a minibus, a white minibus in the dark. It looks like the whiteness of the minibus is being concentrated and then sprayed out like a laser in the beams of broadening white light that emerge from its front.

All the nuances of the valley – the farmhouses, the barbed-wire fences, the long rows in straight lines that curve with the contours – all of those are just different shades of darkness. And so the light doesn't do much, it doesn't get very far into it. But it's there, unmissable in the lightless vista.

And the people on board, and the drinks they are drinking, slosh around as the road winds and roughens. But it goes on, the minibus.

There is a man looking out of the window. He has had to press his face right up to the window because otherwise all he could see was the reflection of the inside, hanging spectrally in the air.

The minibus is divided into seats grouped together in different combinations, because there's no central aisle, you just get on in the middle. There are twos and threes and ones.

And Tam has ended up with a one, which he doesn't mind because he doesn't know anyone else.

The others on the bus are a bit younger than him maybe. Not by loads but he feels it a bit. Maybe he just feels how time has passed for him. Now is now, but it will soon be Then.

Tam sometimes tries to really focus in on the Now, to experience it, cling on to it, before it slips away into Then. He is not sure if that makes time pass faster or slower. Slower because you dive deep down into each part of it. Faster because what you dive down deep into is the slipping away.

He is gazing out into the valley of darkness.

Then a voice at the back says, 'Hey, isn't it you Tam?'

He hears her saying to her friend that they used to work together.

Tam pulls his face from the window. Now is now, he thinks.

'He seemed a quiet one!' Another voice.

Tam thinks maybe Now is something you have to engage with there and then and maybe Then is something you already engaged with, or that you can choose to ignore or suppress.

A man across the aisle says to Tam, 'Do you want a beer pal?'

Another man says: 'We're nearly out.'

'There'll be more there,' says the beer offerer.

Tam takes a moment. As he answers he moves his hand to his inside pocket so that he can feel the rectangular shape he's put there.

'Yeah go on then,' Tam says. Then he makes himself smile because he read once that if you make yourself smile your body thinks you are smiling for real and it makes you feel better. And it made him feel strange about smiling after that. But he smiles and he takes the beer and he feels the smile and the smile of the beer offerer too.

Tam says his name. The woman at the back is called Annie and she says her name. Many more names flow forward from everyone sitting around them.

Tam says 'Well I won't remember all those' and everyone laughs. And after he says that the minibus bumps a little chunkily through a pothole and everyone bounces and they laugh again about that.

Soon the minibus slows and comes to a gravelly halt. The slowing down brings a quiet, the passengers reminded of the night outside of the cocoon in which they have been carried.

There's a grouping of a few houses, lonely sentinels in the nothingness.

The road beyond this point is supposed to be closed. There's a sign saying so, and a half-hearted roadblock. A barrel and some wire and a bit of fence and some rocks.

The driver gets out and talks to a man and a boy. The boy brings a series of crates to the back of the minibus. The driver and the man talk for a while. Tam sees the driver slip him a big thick wad of cash.

There is light coming into the minibus now from the houses. Tam slips the rectangular case out of his pocket. Just a little cardboard case, protective but not permanent-feeling. The case isn't important really, he thinks. But sometimes he thinks maybe it needs to be stronger and why hasn't he got a stronger one. Something waterproof maybe. He opens it up. The photo is still there. Of course. But there's a relief every time, that it has not been inexplicably lost.

He takes the photo out of the case, the tips of his fingers on the edges of the photo. It sits on the palm of his hand like a boat sits delicately on the water.

15

The corners of the photo are curling backwards, downwards. Like they are trying to get away, like the photo belongs to the depths and is trying to return there. Or maybe it is that the middle of the photo, where all the people are, is trying to get forward, like the people are trying to get towards him, to flee from the depths.

Tam is afraid of the curl. Because the curl, distinct from the perfect flat rectangle of the photo as it had been, is another kind of decline.

A couple more men, big men, come out and Tam thinks he sees one of them holding a gun in the gloom. They tie one end of a rope around part of the rock in the roadblock, and the other end to a jeep. There's the sound of some scraping, some moving of heaviness. The minibus rumbles, then edges forward. Shadows flit across the van, diagonally and briefly, as the light from the houses slips away.

Tam folds the case and puts the photo back in his inside pocket.

After a while the road dips down a little. The tide is low and they know it is distant, but as the minibus ploughs through puddles the sound of the water hushes its passengers.

'How have you been then Tam?' Maybe she is his age, he thinks.

Annie has orchestrated a seat swap so that she's in a two and she has got Tam to sit next to her.

She worked for his dad. Part of the Scottish wine industry which is still recent enough that it should be burgeoning, but is now, like so many things, decaying. What was her role? he thinks. He can't remember.

He thought some people didn't like his dad because he worked them hard. He never cared much for that. But he felt trapped between the two worlds, his dad the boss and the staff who were like him and not like him. He wonders if she dislikes him or if she has realised she remembers him better than he does her.

'It's been ages, years,' she says.

His dad was all right to people really, he thinks. Firm but fair.

'Oh you know,' Tam says. 'Hard times right. Same for everyone.'

Tam smiles, to try to express something like: What can you do.

'Yeah.' She pauses. 'Yeah, hard times. Are you still in the wine game?'

'Sort of. A bit, yeah. I work for Mr Griffin now actually. And yourself?'

'Oh really. Didn't expect that. But . . .'

She hesitates, seems to change what she was going to say.

'I'm not in wine anymore either. There's not much left is there. I'm up in the city now. Bit of teaching, bars, that kind of thing.'

Mr Griffin had been Tam's father's old competitor. They had always had a rivalry, and Tam had always thought it had been quite bitter. So it did seem surprising he worked for him now, he thought sometimes.

But maybe, Tam thinks, maybe he just doesn't see me as a threat now. Or maybe there just hadn't been the time for a proper old family feud to build up. The Scottish wine industry was hardly ancient, after all. And Mr Griffin probably thought Tam would have his father's winemaking genes.

Doug said he'd never work for him. But Tam didn't mind so much, not now.

Maybe Mr Griffin had meant what he'd said when he had said: 'And no offence meant to you, but I feel sorry for you.'

And he'd given him a job, some fairly cursory role in the business, and Tam would sit in an office, an office which stood quite high at the top of a ridge, overlooking the gentle, deadly valley.

And his boss would say 'We're looking at new land in Iceland, and some of the foothills of Norwegian fjords.' And 'There's too many floods in Scotland now. And the climate is getting too unpredictable.'

And Tam would remember his father having said things like that, aware of the precariousness of their own vineyards, as the coast crept up on them and the weather buffeted them and sometimes blew things away or drowned them. He'd had to sell some, to focus on the rest. He said that the summer sun, getting more brutal and relentless each year, would parch the land, weaken it. The rains and the winds and the floods would sweep that weakness away.

And eventually one of the big sweeping erosions did take the last key bits of their land, and a flood took the rest of that year's harvest, and what his father had worked for. And his father couldn't stand it, because he'd put all the love he could no longer give to Tam's mother into those fields, from the first fields in the Borders, to the Highlands, a thousand acres we'd had at one point, Doug used to say to him, and look at us now.

Tam thinks this and misses the beat of the conversation and realises he hasn't said anything about what Annie said but he says: 'Oh cool.'

Annie says: 'Cheap to live there really, plenty of room. Not too chaotic, not too violent. Not since things have calmed down. I'm just down here for this.'

There's another silence and there's a question that nobody dares ask anyone: Are you alone? What happened to the others?

Part of Tam wants to get the photo out. It's not the right time.

'I saw Doug actually, maybe a year or so back,' says Annie.

Tam thinks: The last couple of years have been quite stable in general, all things considered. The waves of novel malarias and fevers that swept in with the rising sea levels and the heat are under control now. The towns are more orderly. Apparently the death rates aren't too far off what they were before, if the news is right. It is fair to think it was a safe question. But he doesn't say anything.

She says: 'He looked well.'

Tam takes a deep breath through his nose and purses his lips tight into a straight line.

'I'm sorry,' he says, 'Doug went last year.'

'Ah Tam I'm so sorry.'

Doug was the last to go. He died in the valley by the new estuary, close to where Tam still lives.

The tides weren't as consistent as they used to be. Historically water flows over the same bits of land for centuries, millennia, longer. And so in those instances the water wears away the bits that can be worn away, and the other bits stay. And the water finds its routes, and in the lifetime of one human, or several generations of them, not much changes. People get to know when it is safe and when it is not.

But now there is a great inconsistency. And the estuaries stretch much further than they used to, over land that has not always known the depths. And so it depends on how the rain

19

has been in the weeks before, or where or when else there have been new flows, or big flows, or big melts.

And so sometimes the tides come rushing in much faster, right down quick along the valley, a relentless marching army, and they are not averse to finding new ground.

His brother was out there, one of the scavengers. He'd always been the industrious one, and their father had eventually entrusted him more with the mechanics of running the vineyards.

Tam remembers that his father always said: 'We were the first Scottish wine growers, and we're the best.'

His father had grown up in France and then he moved north, decades ago, first northern England, and then he struck out alone, further north still. The land he got was cheap but for good reason, it turned out. And eventually it had all sunk away.

And so Tam's brother was out there on the brackish hinterland, a scavenger instead. An upcycler he called it.

He had been doing quite well, Doug, he had his father's knack for hard work and he had a wronged hunger of a man who wanted back what he had lost.

Doug had said to Tam that he could see how the whole sorry upcycling industry worked and it didn't work fantastic. Maybe he'd try giving it a proper go himself, start his own company, get some people in to work for him instead of working for someone else. There's a lot of valuable stuff out there half-buried. If we do it better, faster, smarter we could make more.

But at that point he was still down at the bottom rung, riffling through the mire himself.

And there is so much heaviness bound up in that water, in

that sludge, in all the space it flows over. Old industrial units, farm buildings, houses, all full of wires and weeds and long tentacles of metal. All slurped over with mud, all boggy and sticky, and even that just hides the jagged entangling truths.

So you can get stuck, or get snarled up in something old and metal, or you can just be too far from anything that ends up above the waterline. And so the tide came in. And they found his body a few days later, all bloated, pallid, suddenly unindustrious.

This is how Tam understands it.

He doesn't say that though. He says: 'Yeah. Drowned in the estuary. I'm the family now.' And that second sentence answers the unsaid question.

Tam thinks: Can you be a family of one?

Annie says: 'Tam I'm so sorry.' She puts her arm around him, a sort of half hug, and as the minibus sways around a corner their bodies come together more firmly.

She says, 'I'm so sorry Tam. Doug told me about the others.'

They sit in silence a bit longer. Tam thinks it is his responsibility to either ask Annie about her situation or to change the subject. And then someone says: 'We're nearly there.'

They hear it before they see it. An unmistakable low thudding, rumbling. It sounds primitive and unsophisticated from afar, just loose noise adrift on the wind.

Ahead of Tam someone is explaining the curfew dust to someone who must be down from the city too. Because you're not supposed to go out into the countryside or the lost towns and villages at night, the authorities spray green curfew dust up into the air. It drifts out over the abandoned towns

21

and villages. If it gets on anyone's clothes they sparkle with it and it's impossible to get it off, sometimes ever, watch out for that, he's saying. They use it as evidence apparently.

There's none now, but Tam sees it often, a bit less than there used to be, but pretty often it's there, wisping through the air. Sometimes the wind changes and it comes back the wrong way. Tam isn't sure it was ever very effective, but they still do it. They started doing it when the curfews came in, like they started doing so many things. And they just haven't stopped.

But it's not so hard to get around the curfew really. These kinds of parties happen often enough. Although Tam hasn't been for a long while now. It feels different and it feels familiar.

Tam got this minibus, the late one, because he wanted it to be in full swing when he arrived. No hanging around, because he was going by himself. Now Annie is there, and her friends. He is glad about that.

They had never really spoken much, Tam and Annie. He would always have been just kicking around, not sure whether he was pretending at the job or whether the job and the world of work entirely consisted of pretending. Doug would pick up the slack of the actual work.

Off the bus there's a bit of a buzz. The beer offerer is saying: 'You don't get many proper parties in the towns anymore. Not allowed. Too easy to shut down when they try. You have to come out to things like this.'

A rig has been assembled. There are maybe a couple of hundred people in and around the church.

There's a DJ where the priest would usually stand, and the decks are on what would have been the altar. There's a few

22

old long bench pews pushed out to the side, and where they would have been there is a dance floor.

About half the roof is gone, revealing the night sky above. But the clouds overhead encase the whole scene tightly.

Annie says do you want something. For dancing.

He says OK, and she gives him it, and he has a swig of beer to wash it down.

'There's supposed to be Northern Lights these weeks apparently,' she says.

'And it's a full moon too,' one of Annie's friends adds.

'We know that, that's the whole point,' says Annie. 'The closest full moon to midsummer.'

They all look up, through the protruding blackened tibias and fibulas of the half-roof. But they can't see anything much, no full moon, no Northern Lights, not even stars, because the clouds cover it all up.

Someone had said on the bus, We are all fucking pagans going to a party because of the moon. He was laughing. He was going as well so it was hardly much of a critique.

The last festival on earth they called it.

'An exaggeration but not by much,' someone had said.

In the transept they've set up a little kind of bar, with the beers from the minibus and from all the other buses and cars that had pushed through the darkness to get there.

Annie goes there and Tam says he'll go and dance right away, and he does.

He sees a familiar old face, someone without a name, who doesn't know his. And the familiar face says: 'All right! Ain't seen you in a while,' and they hug.

And Tam is at the front, past the people chatting on the fringes of the crowd, to the front where no one really notices him slipping alongside them, all lost in the sound, unextractable from the moment. Tam's feeling nothing for now, waiting for it all to wash over him, but the sound is warm and powerful and makes him move, and he does, his body moving with other bodies, just a gentle tingle, the bass pouring through him.

It goes on, and he has dug right down into the music and does not even notice whether it is Now or Then, or what has happened or what will happen.

Annie comes over with a group. Tam just wants to dance, and so does she.

Tam thinks he can hear different words in the beats. He half mutters that to Annie and she smiles. The beer offerer from the coach offers Tam another beer, a man with seemingly unlimited access to beer, Tam laughs and tells him, and he laughs too. The can opens with a satisfying spray.

The dancing goes on. Tam wants to repay the beer offerer's favours. On his way to the bar someone in the pews is reading from a tatty paperback to a small group. She sits on the top of the backrest with her feet on the seat and Tam hears:

> 'I practised love carelessly
> And I had little patience for nature's beauty.
> So passed my time
> Given to me on earth.'

Tam is back, he gives out beers like a returning champion and says to the beer offerer 'I am you now.'

He knows that Now is fleeting, artificial even, that it will pass – but it is real too, it is something, and he feels it, this moment exists. He is telling Annie this. She is smiling.

And then, for a moment, just a moment, through the roof, the clouds clear, and the sky is filled with sparkle, and the curfew dust mingles in with the Aurora Borealis, and the stars, and the full moon, impossibly bright, and the sound swelling, and the church bells ring. Every hour they ring the bells of the church and you can go outside by the fire and join a ceremony, but Tam stays at the front, dancing, exchanging smiles, the music is good.

Tam goes to where the toilets are, just two portaloos set back a little from the church building. Somehow it still doesn't feel right to piss on a church. There's a small queue. In it, a man, hair askew, a sort of rag-bandanna around his neck, starts to talk. Tam isn't sure if he is trying to strike up conversation with him or if he is mad or drunk or high or what.

The man says: 'We went to the fucking edge once, most weirdest time of my life, digging into the mud like a wader bird, scrambling and combing for worms and shopping trolleys.'

And he says: 'You get paid half for getting the coins out of the trolley and half goes to your gangmaster – they make millions a year.'

Tam thinks maybe he should just go and piss against a bush or tree.

The man says: 'It's a scam. They're in league with the supermarkets, they could make the trolleys free but they need their coins at the bottom of the riverbed when the tide is low.'

And Tam nods, looks away. Just a rambling man, talking about nothing that makes any sense, but it's made Tam think too much. The man drifts off into the crowd. Maybe he wasn't even queuing. Tam goes to the toilet. When he comes out he looks off into the crowd, can't see anyone.

He feels out of sync with the mood. He takes a seat in the

church facing towards the altar. There is a tinge of morning in the distance through the empty windows.

He thinks about going outside to the fire.

He sits there a while, mulling it over. He didn't come here to think about the state of the world too much, but it was important to be here. It was at one of these parties that they had met.

He's thinking about it but he doesn't want to.

One of Annie's friends from the bus passes him. Not the beer offerer, but someone else.

'You all right Tam?'

Tam says, 'I told you this would happen, but I'm sorry – I've forgotten your name.'

They both laugh. He tells Tam his name again and says 'Do you want a beer? I was on my way to the bar.'

Tam stands up. 'I'll come with you.'

It's good to stand and walk together. They get their beers, and the beers taste good, crisp. A bit of energy. They lean on the wall looking at the dance floor, the rhythm going through them.

And then he hears something familiar. They've put on a song. It was her favourite song.

Tam stands forward, energised again now.

Tam says to Annie's friend, 'This was her favourite.'

He says 'Shall we go and dance to it then with the others?' Tam says 'You go ahead I'll dance here. I'll join you later.'

And Tam dances on his own, where the nave meets the crossing, away from the mass of the dance floor, and he is looking up, in this abandoned but not collapsed church, in these dark times, the music still exists, and so does he.

He looks up, there are little gaps in the clouds with a star or two, and the curfew dust seems thick now, sparkling in between heaven and the ground, and he repeats, to no one, 'This was her favourite.'

And it is the last song and the music is finished now, and the sun is mostly up, and those that remain, that haven't taken their bus back yet, they drift gently outside to sit by the fire, aglow.

And the bells ring one last time.

And everyone takes out their own photos from wherever they have kept them safely.

And each person stands in turn and says the names of those in their photo and holds up the photo, the last ceremony of the night.

And it is Tam's turn and he says his name and he says:

'My mother Ruth, in the sicknesses.

'My fiancée Sara, in the sicknesses.' (She would be forever suspended in that potential.)

'My father, Emmanuel. Suicide.

'My brother, Doug. He drowned in the estuary. One year ago today.

'I am Tam. I am still here. I am alive.'

And people take him by the hand. And he gazes into the fire, and they walk him around, once for his mother, once for his fiancée, once for his father, once for his brother. And people hug and Annie holds his hand as they sit down, and he feels just good about that, to be there, alone but not alone.

This is what we have now, this is what we had before.

And it is someone else's turn, and then someone else. Some of Annie's friends, familiar faces now. And then it is someone else's turn. And then it is Annie's turn. Everyone's face is bright now, the day has really begun, the sun has really

27

risen, again, as it always does.

And afterwards Tam gazes out. The dawn shows the ground around the church all churned up by the footprints of the night, into mud and water, into abstract shapes in which Tam thinks he can see faces.

And in the still little puddles of groundwater and dew and beer and piss there is the impression of the sky in miniature, over and over again, the stars and moon and the Aurora Borealis all gone, replaced by the all-consuming light of day, a warm silvery embrace. But the green smudge of the dust still lingers, made softer and more diffuse by the passing of time and the wind, but sparkling still, giving the whole scene a quiet shimmer. The reverberating wake of the flood of the night, in which they have all gone under, and from which they are now emerging, blinking, wide-eyed, changed and the same, a new day, again.

Fix

K. Lockwood Jefford

A teenager goes missing from a seaside town. By the time his disappearance is reported to police, he's not been seen for three days. At least not by anyone in his family.

Before the city across the estuary reached out with its award-winning suspension bridge and seized it as a suburb on its western edge, a dormitory for commuters, the seaside town was its own place. A pebbly beach, a pretty esplanade, a pier restored with EU money long before the referendum, an international sixth-form college perched on the cliff.

A Local Enterprise Partnership has been established, with a Local Industrial Strategy. There are plans for a new football stadium on an old landfill site and – the pet project of the deputy leader of the city council – a clifftop complex with commercial units and a creative hub of workshops and studios for letting at subsidised rents to artists with proven financial need. The fate of the old maternity hospital, a grey-stone Gothic Grade II listed building, is out to tender.

House prices have risen, rents increased, the retired population has swelled. Teenagers hang about on street corners or dodge the expensive fares on buses over the bridge to the city.

*

The teenager's sister is in her late twenties and lives near the city end of the bridge in a studio flat bought by her parents. She paints portraits of small children brought to model by doting mums and dads. She watches the traffic zipping both ways along the bridge's four-lane highway like electric beetles, the racket rasping at her ears like a cloud of raging hornets. Sometimes she blocks it out by listening to music through headphones. This is what she was doing the day she had six missed calls from her brother.

The area around the massive concrete slab anchoring the bridge to the seaside town becomes a destination for drug drops and dealing.

Some months previously, police stopped a van being driven over the bridge with a known drug dealer as a passenger. The driver, a thirty-one-year-old unemployed hospital porter, tried to flee but gave up on realising his only escape route was a fifty-metre drop into the estuary.

In court, the ex-porter admits to driving a man who supplied drugs. His counsel states he'd pleaded guilty at an early stage, that at the time he'd been addicted to heroin and his relationship had recently broken up. The judge says the drug dealer couldn't operate without his help and that an immediate sentence is justified.

A consultant psychiatrist in her early forties arrives for the clinic she runs from a Portakabin in the grounds of the city's hospital. The clinic where she sees the teenager for the mood swings he self-medicates with illicit drugs.

The consultant's secretary hands her an armful of case notes and points at a headline in the local paper: *Ex Hospital Porter Jailed 18 Months*. Beneath, a photograph of a man with small black eyes in a sickly-looking face set somewhere between tearful and telling you to fuck off. Her secretary is excited because the ex-porter used to work at the hospital's sterile-supplies department until he was sacked for stealing surgical gloves. The consultant doesn't recognise him. She feels the first stabs of a headache, takes two of the dihydrocodeine she keeps in her desk drawer and opens the teenager's file.

She has been seeing him for a few months since his parents' BUPA insurance ran out for the Priory. Typically, he skips along to his appointments late, neck swathed in silky scarves, long hair swept up in a ponytail, fingernails painted blue, fishnet tights peeping out from under skinny jeans. He talks about his life in an upbeat way, insists the six-inch scar on the inside of his left forearm is due to an accident with the bread knife.

His mother does something in the art world and the father's a senior civil servant. They are in their fifties, and have a huge house in the seaside town where the teenager attends the expensive sixth-form college. It was the school that raised concerns about his poor attendance and failing performance. A sister died in a traffic accident when he was only seven. He says his mother hasn't smiled since. Another sister lives in the city so it's just him with his parents at home. They're old, he says.

They don't know about the heroin he buys off the dark web.

The teenager's sister sees the report and the ex-porter's name rings alarm bells. She Googles it and finds a newspaper report of her sister's death ten years ago: *Motorcyclist Responsible For Death Of Talented Teen*. It's the same name but a different address in the seaside town. The dilapidated bit behind the old maternity hospital. She calls her mother who asks if her brother is there.

A trainee psychiatrist who works in the consultant's team sees the ex-porter's picture and recognises him as the man he was called to see a week ago on the medical ward. The man had come in by ambulance, whining and writhing about, complaining of pain all over his body. He was keeping patients with serious medical conditions awake, they said. It was murder to find a vein, but all the blood tests were normal. A heroin addict, they said, nothing medically wrong with him, but his girlfriend had thrown him out and there were no hostel places or crisis beds. We can't just let him go, they said.

The trainee remembers the man's papery skin all shades of grey and blue, etched with scars and track marks barely hidden by botched DIY tattoos. Waves of sobbing shook his flimsy body, which looked as if it limped from fix to fix, got itself kicked, punched and bashed about. His sunken belly gurgled like water pipes. He was trying to sort himself out, he said. He'd rowed with his girlfriend. His drugs counsellor was off sick, he had a court case coming up and couldn't get hold of his solicitor. He'd felt so bad he started punching the walls. His head. Then he got the pains all over.

The trainee knows they hate people like him clogging up beds. He arranged a transfer to the mental health unit and prescribed plenty of sedation. The nurses called in the morning to say he'd discharged himself.

*

The teenager doesn't turn up for his appointment or answer his phone when the consultant calls. Her headache intensifies, untouched by the painkillers. An email marked URGENT! drops into her inbox. *All consultants must attend a consultation on reorganisation of mental health services.* She knows 'reorganisation' means cuts forced by years of austerity and, in her view, 'consultation' is a box-ticking farce. We hear what you're saying. Thank you for attending.

She writes herself a prescription for tramadol and slips out to a different chemist to the one she used a few days ago.

Police officers ask for consent to search the teenager's home for any evidence or leads as to why he has gone. This is normal procedure. Police officers ask the teenager's parents for consent to make public the fact he is missing. The parents don't have a recent photograph, but the teenager's sister has a selfie the teenager sent her, taken when he was high on heroin. A smile lifts his face, the corners of his mouth, brightens his eyes.

The teenager's mother tells police it's not unusual to not see him for a few days. Both she and her husband have intensive careers that demand time and focus. Ultimately, their children benefit. Private schools. Travel. Her son often visits his sister, a talented artist, in the city. She had assumed he was there. They are a very close family, especially since another daughter died in a tragic road accident ten years ago. She was only sixteen.

It appears the teenager's father was the last person to have seen his son. He tells the police his wife was in bed and he was working on his laptop at the kitchen table. His son came in for a drink of water. He doesn't tell them his son saw he was masturbating. He tells the police they didn't speak. Which is true.

The missing teenager's disappearance is reported in the local paper and on radio and television news programmes. The police issue a statement to say they are concerned for his welfare and are urgently appealing for help from the public to trace him. There is a special phone number to call. A reference number to quote.

The missing teenager's picture is on page two. The front page carries a photograph of the deputy leader of the city council shaking hands with a local entrepreneur who has a major stake in the new football stadium.

The service director tells the consultant she must attend the consultation meeting even though it means she will have to cancel a clinic. He tells her there is a serious proposal to build a new mental health unit on the site of the old maternity hospital in the seaside town. He says this is fantastic news for her.

The old maternity hospital is where the consultant's son was born by emergency caesarean section. They did everything they could to save him, but it wasn't enough.

The baby would have been five years old next month.

She believes she wasn't cut out to be a mother. Her husband thinks she'll change her mind. He doesn't know she's taking the contraceptive pill. She places two tramadol on her tongue, swigs her bottled water to wash them down.

*

The ex-porter sees the missing teenager's picture. It triggers flashbacks of the girl. Looks just like her. That night. Ten years ago. Girlfriend was right pissed off with him because he forgot to pick up the chips for their tea. Sent him straight back out. He'd zapped down to the takeaway, didn't see the girl. It was January, foggy, frosty. Yamaha brakes were dodgy. He didn't see her.

Felt her though.

Did four months inside for death by careless driving. When he came out he had no job. He'd felt like shit. Couldn't sleep. Lost weight. His relationship was on its last legs and he didn't want to lose access to his kids. His doctor prescribed valium. But he felt pathetic taking a woman's pill, so he stopped. It was his uncle gave him his first hit. Have some of this. You'll feel warm and nice.

His relationship fell apart. The next one didn't last either. He lost contact with his kids. Couldn't stick any of the crappy jobs he got. Heroin stayed. At first it numbed over the bad stuff and let some good squeeze through. But it got harder to squeeze, to stay the right side of sick as a dog. His uncle said, Take more, no problem. Only a tenner a hit. Then it was, Inject, it works faster. Have one on me for free.

Too distracted to paint, the missing teenager's sister cancels all her portrait clients and Googles 'missing teenagers' instead. She finds herself scrolling through screen after screen after screen:

> *A nine-year-old boy and a fourteen-year-old*
> *girl go missing after a trip to the library.*

Police launch a search for a thirteen-year-old girl, last seen leaving her home at 6 p.m. on the 10th of November. Police are growing increasingly concerned for her welfare.

Police are appealing for information to help find a fifteen-year-old boy last seen at 4 p.m. on 6th February leaving a friend's house. He is described as white, five feet four inches tall, of slim build, with brown hair and wearing a grey hooded top and dark jeans. Officers are becoming increasingly concerned for his welfare and ask anyone who has seen him or knows where he is to call police quoting this reference number.

Two teenagers aged sixteen and seventeen are found safe and well. Police will not release the location of where they were found.

After an extensive police search and campaign by family friends, the girl's body was discovered at a quarry close to her home. Her family released a statement asking for privacy. Police say there are no suspicious circumstances.

A missing teen's body was found six days after he went missing from home.

A thirteen-year-old was found dead yesterday, nine days after disappearing.

The missing teenager's sister sets up a fresh canvas and starts to paint the images inside her.

A car is found abandoned by the concrete slab anchoring the bridge to the seaside town. It is identified as belonging to the missing teenager's father, who didn't know it was missing. DNA found inside doesn't match the missing teenager.

The trainee psychiatrist reads a report in the *British Journal of Psychiatry* that suggests suicide has overtaken road traffic accidents as the major cause of death in fifteen- to twenty-five-year-olds. He is determined to make a difference in his chosen profession.

When he attends supervision with the consultant, he sees a pile of the *British Journal of Psychiatry* as high as her desk, still wrapped in their cellophane sheaths.

The consultant was on the trainee's interview panel, where he'd described being 'passionate about mental health'. This had impressed the service director, but the consultant is concerned about people who say they are 'passionate about mental health'. It's a job, she thinks. Be passionate about other things.

A body is found in the estuary. It is not the missing teenager.

In prison, the ex-porter gets pains all over his body. No physical cause can be found. He is seen by the visiting forensic psychiatrist who takes a detailed history and says the pain is psychological and that his family had no language for emotion. The ex-porter disagrees. He tells the psychiatrist his family did have a language for emotion, only not in words. The last time he saw his mother she tipped him off a chair like he was a bag of rubbish.

The psychiatrist puts him on one-to-one suicide watch and refers him to the hospital wing. The referral gets stuck as there are no free officers to escort him.

The missing teenager's body is found in undergrowth near a clifftop path by police. Postmortem examination reveals the cause of death was hypothermia. The coroner is notified.

The service director calls the consultant in the middle of a clinic to tell her. There will be a routine Serious Incident Inquiry, of course, he says.

She excuses herself and rushes to the toilet where she sits in a cubicle and cries so hard her head hurts as if her skull will split. She should have seen it coming. He was only eighteen for Christ's sake. Somebody knocks on the door to ask if she's OK.

Afterwards her eyeballs feel like they've been rolled in grit.

At the Serious Incident Inquiry, the consultant describes how she tried to engage the teenager, how she believed he was depressed beneath his upbeat veneer. A false self, a defence, she says. She was concerned when he didn't attend his appointment and had tried to contact him. She had not been in contact with his parents in treatment as he'd asked her not to. He'd given his sister as next of kin. It's a fine balance, she says, managing the clinical risk and maintaining rapport. It's all detailed in his risk plan. He was eighteen. If I'd spoken to his parents about him without his consent, I could have ruptured the therapeutic relationship.

In her interview for the Inquiry, the teenager's sister says he'd had a row with their parents about running up thousands of pounds on his mother's credit card, buying stuff from Gucci.

Their parents didn't have a clue about the drugs, she says. He said they helped numb over the bad mood swings, calmed him. But it got harder and he needed more and more. He had to get a dealer. Then she'd found him on the toilet in her bathroom peeing like a girl. He had a syringe in his teeth, a scarf tied tight around his arm and he was slapping his vein, going, Come on. One more fix. She didn't know it'd got that bad and threatened to tell their parents. He pleaded with me not to, she says. Promised he was going to the clinic and the consultant was going to get him on a treatment programme as soon as a place came up.

The teenager's parents lodge a complaint about the service received by their son, citing 'lack of communication and confidentiality taken too far'. They say he should have been admitted.

The service director emails the consultant about the complaint. *Please review notes ASAP esp. concerning crisis and contingency plans so I can write a response.*

The consultant sees the email on her phone while she is attending a presentation about reorganising mental health services in line with evidence-based data. She takes an extra tramadol.

That evening her husband prepares a special dinner to mark their tenth wedding anniversary, which she has forgotten. Afterwards he tries to persuade her to come to bed and she tells him she won't be long. She tweets about the fetishisation of data which is idealised so managers making cuts to services feel justified. Feel better. Inured. *The reality is we need properly trained, experienced staff to see complex cases. Instead, services are put out to tender to the cheapest bidder.*

At 4 a.m. she wakes on the sofa with a cricked neck and throbbing head.

The teenager's sister reads the report from the Serious Incident Inquiry. It says, *When she was found she was blue.* She doesn't know why the report says 'she' in several places.

To her, her brother always looked like a boy who looked like a girl who looked like a boy.

The teenager's mother is interviewed by the local press. Services for soaring numbers of young people who have self-harmed or are having some sort of breakdown are grossly inadequate, she says. It prolongs suffering for children and their families.

She tells the reporter that she and her husband and daughter are closer than ever in grief.

The local entrepreneur's son gets a studio in the creative hub despite having an income well above the minimum wage from a job in the company run by his uncle.

*

The teenager's sister watches the traffic on the bridge at night. A glimmering necklace of ruby gemstones on the left, a string of shimmering diamonds on the right.

The mental health service relocates to a new unit at the old maternity hospital. It is cold and smells of plastic. Files are lost in transition. Two staff leave and their posts are frozen.

The teenager's parents announce they are setting up their own charity for young people with mental health and drug problems.

The trainee psychiatrist goes to see the teenager's sister's exhibition at the new clifftop complex. A series of abstract portraits called Missing.

He buys a painting. It is more than he can really afford. The teenager's sister smiles, thanks him, places a red dot on the canvas.

The consultant's application to sit on a panel advising the Local Enterprise Partnership on services for young people with mental health problems is blocked.

The head of procurement at the local NHS trust is under investigation for receiving VIP tickets and hospitality from a bidding company during a tender process for converting the old maternity hospital into a specialist mental health unit.

A twenty-one-year-old man with a long history of substance misuse while in prison dies after he sets himself on fire when smoking drugs in his cell. A thirty-one-year-old man who had previously self-harmed in jail, and had been assessed as having an increased risk of suicide, is found hanged in his cell.

Cracks are found on the road surface of the bridge. It is closed for investigation. The consultant's drive to work is increased by five miles and fifty minutes in the morning rush hour.

A teenager goes missing.

Small Differences

Huma Qureshi

Tasneem stood barefoot on the antique terracotta flagstones of the kitchen, grateful for their piercing coolness. Outside the heat was stifling. The air, unmoving, was pressing and making it hard for her to read and so she had offered to go in and make iced tea. Simon teased her for her inability to withstand temperatures over twenty-five degrees, as if her heritage somehow meant she was supposed to be immune. She pointed out the illogic of his reason – she had never lived in the Indian subcontinent, she had not even been there since she was twelve – and then he softened, telling her he thought it was sweet, that was all. She stood up and stretched. It was too hot to come up with a retort, especially within earshot of his parents, so she rolled her eyes at him and walked away.

In the shade of the kitchen, she held an ice cube to her forehead, her hairline clammy. She let it trickle down her neck as she set the tea to brew and sliced up the last punnet of soft strawberries remaining in the fridge. They would have to buy more food and the thought of having to make an excursion to the town market with Simon's parents, of everything taking twice as long as they deliberated over what to buy and what to eat, irritated her. She told herself it was the intensity of the

43

heat, that Simon did not ordinarily bristle her like this. But they had been in Tuscany for five days and halfway through, their holiday already felt too long.

Tasneem heard the slap of Simon's flip-flops upon the floor as he entered through the garden doors but she did not turn around. She felt him behind her, his warm hands holding her waist, his face nestled into her bare shoulder.

'I'm sorry,' he said.

'You know, you're not that funny. It's hot. I hate it. Big deal. OK?' Tasneem said, still without turning around.

'I'm sorry,' he said again and then he kissed her shoulder, spun her to face him and pulled her close. 'I love you,' he murmured into her hair and she let him hold her for just a moment but then she pushed him away.

'Too hot for all this nonsense too,' she said.

She topped up the jug of tea with a blast of cold water, tossed in yet more ice. She placed the bowl of strawberries upon a tray along with glasses and the jug and as she carried it out she shook her head.

'Hey, let me,' Simon said but she had already stepped out of the door and set the tray down upon the low wicker table on the terrace. Simon followed her under the shade of the veranda and lightly touched the small of her back, a gesture to show he would take over, and so she sat down on a worn sunlounger as he poured two glasses of iced tea. 'Here you are,' he said and then he passed a glass each to his father, his mother. His parents were talking about the weather, how they had not seen a summer so hot in the hills before. Tasneem waited but when Simon then pulled out his phone to check a more detailed weather report, she poured a glass of iced tea of her own. 'Oh,' Simon said, looking up at her. 'Sorry,

44

sweetheart, I thought you had yours already.'

In the late afternoon, they drove to the farmers' market in the neighbouring town square to pick up supplies. Tasneem and Simon sat in the back and Simon reached for her hand, placing it in his lap like a teenager, while his father drove and his mother sat in the passenger seat. It occurred to Tasneem as she looked out the window through her sunglasses at the passing scenes, the sunflowers edging the country lanes, the olive groves far off in the distance, that she had never sat in the back of her parents' car holding hands with a boy like this. From time to time Simon's mother twisted around in her seat to smile at them and Simon squeezed her fingers a little tighter.

Upon arrival at the market Simon's parents planned a menu, counting off the remaining meals left to prepare for the week on their fingers. They ambled past stalls, taking their time to choose breads, cheeses and fresh pasta hanging in strips like shoelaces. In spite of her initial irritation at having to do this, Tasneem found herself relaxing. The afternoon sun was still hot but the air was lighter now, the market livelier today than it had been before. The stalls were set out in the town square under the shade of a biscuit-coloured church, crumbling and spectacular. Today the church doors were unlocked and tourists wandered in and out seeking cool respite under its high holy ceilings. Stall owners jostled with passers-by, tempting them with ragged squares of bread to dip into sweet sharp vinegars, holding out small dishes of cubes of strong warm cheese and pitted olives to try. Tasneem marvelled at the size of plump tomatoes as large as the palm of her hand, took a bite out of a ripe, soft peach that an old

45

man with a withered face almost as nut-brown as hers offered as a gift. Simon put his arm around her shoulders and she raised her hand up to meet his, their fingers clasped. They walked like this a little way behind his parents and for some time, as they sampled sugared almonds and crunched upon grissini, swapping short kisses in between, Tasneem forgot the annoyance she had felt earlier towards him, not just today but all the other days since they had arrived in Tuscany as well.

Every night, Simon and his parents stayed up late, drinking wine and laughing over a set of family memories which were impossible for her to even begin to learn. 'Oh, it's a long story,' Simon said each time she tried to find a way into the turns of their conversation, or when he did try to explain, his mother or his father interrupted on a tangent and Tasneem was left on the edges again. Last night Tasneem went to bed early and as she brushed her teeth and heard his father's rumbling voice and his mother's laugh so shrill creeping through the walls, she thought she might as well have not been here at all. But in the town square, they walked like lovers and Tasneem told herself that it was only the weather, prickling her skin and parching her mouth, that had been making her feel irritable like this.

When Simon first suggested they take a holiday together to Tuscany, it was a Saturday, late afternoon, and Tasneem was frowning, her head bent over a cookbook as she followed a recipe for gnocchi. Her dough was sticky and she was worried the meal she had planned for their friends, a couple they had met at a wedding, would be spoiled. 'You know, you could just buy gnocchi ready-made,' Simon said. 'It'd be much quicker. No one would know.' Tasneem flicked flour at him. Forty minutes before their friends were due to arrive, after having boiled a fistful of dumplings and found them tasteless, Tasneem asked Simon to run down to the grocery store to pick up something else instead. She was disappointed and felt foolish. She had wanted to make a good impression upon their friends. 'One day, we'll go to Italy,' Simon said in consolation. 'Eat all the gnocchi you like.'

Simon was not like any of the Pakistani boys she had been introduced to by her mother or her mother's friends. Ever since she had moved to London in her mid-twenties, phone numbers of strangers deemed eligible only by virtue of their family origins and respectable jobs were passed along to her like Chinese whispers. She met them after work for coffee, sometimes making it as far as dinner, yet all the while uninterested in the stilted conversation she endured, resenting how much of her time her mother was making her waste. She had hoped that moving to London and starting a career, no matter how fledgling, would free her from the humdrum of her mother's expectations and the gossip of her mother's friends and it angered her that it did not. When she met Simon at a book reading she worked at, he startled her, first with his boyish preppy looks and his smart observations about the book they were there for, and then with the attention he paid to her; the way he smiled at her and laughed with casual determination as he asked for her number before he left. It took him a day to ask her out for dinner and two more dinners until she slept over in his bed. They fell into the rhythm of an early love, lie-ins on Sundays and cosy dinners midweek, texts and emails all day when they were apart at work at opposite ends of the city. Sometimes when she least expected it, while unpacking groceries or sitting together on the sofa choosing a box set or reading in bed next to him, her head resting upon his bare shoulder, his fingers softly stroking her hair as though lightly strumming an instrument, she felt a sharp sting in her heart, a stab of worry, wondering what her mother would think.

Simon brought Italy up again after their friends had left, while they stacked the dishes together. He told her his parents had a summer house in Tuscany, an old villa with a postage stamp of a swimming pool set high in the hills, which they sometimes rented out for the holidays. It had been some time since he had last been. He said he would find out when the house was vacant, certain his parents would not mind. 'We'll be lord and lady of the manor,' he said. 'It'll be just us.' Tasneem felt a thrill and she curled into him as they both studied the calendars on their phones, choosing potential weeks in the summer they could ask for time off from work. She did not yet know what excuse she would come up with to tell her mother, who thought Tasneem worked late three times a week when really she was sleeping over in Simon's flat in Holland Park, around the corner from Daunt Books, to which he had quickly given her a key and a shelf within his wardrobe. That night, as they moved towards each other in bed and Simon murmured of all the beautiful places in Tuscany he wanted her to see, it never occurred to Tasneem that she might feel as though she did not quite belong at Simon's side, even if for only a week, even if under the warmth of the sun in a place where the fireflies danced at night and the scent of lavender hung low in the air.

At the other end of the town square, Tasneem spotted a table crowded with books, antiques and bric-a-brac. She left Simon on the church steps and told him she would come back in ten, twenty minutes. 'Take your time. I'll wait here,' he said, although she had already turned away. The stall was covered in curios; stacks of secondhand books spilling out of fraying baskets, a bowl of swirled-glass marbles, an intricate jewellery box carved from wood. These were the sort of treasured, artful things she saw scattered in the houses of the girls with whom she went to school, girls whose parents were writers and composers and artists with the stability of an inherited wealth that provided them with large houses full of hardback books and private education for all of their children. Tasneem, on the other hand, had worked hard to win a scholarship and her own childhood home was uncluttered and functional. Simon, who also favoured an organised interior and stacked his books neatly behind closed doors, at least had this in common with her mother. But Tasneem was drawn to this chaotic, expensive world of artistic curiosities like a moth to a filament.

She smiled at the stall owner, ran her finger along the rim of a delicate milk-glass lamp as pale as a pearl, held a crystal bowl in her hands, complimenting its cut details. The stall owner was pleasant, settling into an easy conversation with her, a light Italian lilt to her English. Tasneem lingered, passing her hand over a basket of books, and was surprised to discover one she had long ago meant to buy but for some reason or another had never prioritised. Yet here it was in this little market, a nearly new copy of a collection of Italian short stories translated into English. 'My goodness, I've wanted this for ages,' she said to the stall owner. 'It's meant to be.' She smiled as she paid and thanked the stall owner for

49

her time in shy Italian, and then she looked back across the square to the church steps. She squinted but she could not see Simon there. It suddenly felt urgent to her to find him, show him the book and share her excitement at discovering it here; to acknowledge the romance of reading Italian stories while in Italy. It was books after all that had brought them together in the first place. Sometimes, they read aloud to each other in bed and as she narrowed her eyes and raised her hand to her forehead like a sailor to search through the strips of sunlight for him, she was reminded that this was one of the reasons she was so deeply attracted to him; she found she could speak to him of the words that moved her in a way that she had never been able to with anyone else, not without worrying about sounding pretentious, and certainly not with any of the boys her mother tried to introduce her to. She was suddenly impatient to find him and in that moment, more than anything, all she wanted was to run into his arms and say, 'Look! Look what I found!' But she could not see him anywhere. The market was busier, noisier now. The lighter afternoon had drawn even more people out from their air-conditioned holiday lets and a small pale-blue truck had pulled up selling gelato. The cafés edging the square were filling up. She could hear live music playing, a woman singing an Ella Fitzgerald song. Still, she could not see Simon.

She paced the square for what felt like an hour although it was more likely half. She had pulled out her phone numerous times only to find no signal. She held her hand up to shade her eyes from the slanting shafts of afternoon sun and scanned the square once more. She hesitated when she caught sight of the flash of Simon's mother's bright blond hair, bobbing up and down as she talked. There they were, the three of them sat at a small bistro table on bentwood chairs so delicate, Simon's father looked uncomfortable. The café was tucked away in the corner and so Tasneem had not noticed them sooner. She approached and then stopped, for watching them so absorbed in conversation, a mother and a father both besotted with their only son who held court as though he were a prince, Tasneem felt as though she ought to leave them alone, this perfect family so unlike her own. But then she also felt mildly appalled, because his parents were not even supposed to have been here. Simon and Tasneem were meant to have been here alone, just the two of them, but at the last minute his mother had phoned. 'We're at a loose end,' she had said to Simon. She asked if they might tag along. What could Tasneem say, when it was their summer house in the first place, their son she was falling in love with? So when Simon asked her what she thought, she said it was a wonderful idea, that it would be a pleasure to spend more time with his parents, whom she had only briefly met once before. She clutched the book of short stories close to her chest and suddenly, she felt low. All the fizz of sweet excitement and the girlish anticipation she'd felt just moments before, the urgency to show the book she had bought to Simon, share the treasure she had unearthed, had turned sour, flat.

'I asked you to wait,' she said.

He turned around. 'There you are!'

'I asked you to wait.'

'I did. But then you were a little longer than you said you'd be and so we thought we might grab a coffee so . . .' He gestured at the thick mugs on the table, muddied pools of dark coffee peering up from inside.

Simon's mother smiled at her and then tilted her head

towards Simon's father and raised her eyebrows a touch as if to say, 'Lovers' tiff.'

'But I've been looking for you everywhere.'

'OK, I'm sorry, Tas.' Simon stood up and talked slowly. He pulled over an extra chair. 'Let's get you a cold drink, and then we'll head back home. We bought fresh gnocchi for dinner. I thought you'd like it.'

She felt it then. Their sets of pale-grey eyes upon her, innocent and uncomprehending small moons. There it was, the space wide between them. Simon and his parents on one side, and then her on the other. She knew then that it would always be there, this unspoken shore of misunderstanding, this vanity of small differences. The distance that made life so effortless, so easy, for Simon, so that he might take her on holiday with his wealthy parents to their elegant summer house and have her sleep in his flat three times a week, while she had to pretend to her own parents that he did not exist at all. The sort of misunderstanding that meant his father would mistakenly refer to her background as Indian instead of Pakistani or that his mother would continually place the emphasis of her name in the wrong place.

But then a wave of remorse washed weakly over her. Simon loved her. He had brought her to this beautiful place with its faded buildings and sun-drenched fields after all. She set the book of short stories down on the table and sat next to him, touched his knee, then pressed her palms to her face. 'I'm so sorry,' she said with a sigh to all three of them, embarrassed. 'I don't know what's come over me. I'm all out of sorts.'

'It's only the weather,' Simon said, rubbing her back. 'It bothers you, that's all.'

*

After dinner in the garden – plates of creamy gnocchi – Tasneem went up to bed early again. She stayed for a little while at the table, Simon's thumb lightly touching her wrist or else stroking the small of her back as he leaned, legs outstretched, in his chair. When the conversation turned to one cousin's wedding and another's divorce, Tasneem took it as her cue to leave and said goodnight. Simon didn't press her to stay, didn't say sweetly, 'Sit with me for longer,' or 'I'll come to bed soon,' like he did when she'd yawn on his sofa and say, 'I think it's bed for me.' But she didn't mind quite as much as she had done the nights before because ever since they had returned from the market, Simon had been attentive to her. She had offered to help with the cooking but he rubbed her shoulders and brought her a glass of wine and said, 'No, stay, read your book – we've got it all under control,' and all through dinner, which they ate outside under the stars at the garden table lit by citronella candles, he squeezed her knee or touched her arm, her shoulder, her thigh; and so in this way, she felt they were connected again. Upstairs, she looked for the book she had bought but couldn't find it anywhere in their room. She realised then that she must have left it outside in the garden, where she had first started reading it, but she didn't quite have the energy to go back downstairs and smile at Simon's parents just to retrieve it. Simon would bring it in anyway, she thought, as she fell asleep.

Later, in the middle of the night, Tasneem woke startled as a wild thunder ripped the sky apart. A storm had not been mentioned in any of the weather reports Simon and his parents read aloud to each other every day. She sat up in bed and looked over at Simon, his breathing deep and oblivious, his skin luminous in the dark. She didn't know when he'd come in or how long he'd stayed outside, drinking wine with his parents. She hadn't heard him open the door, hadn't felt him slide into bed. He hadn't reached for her waist or kissed her shoulder, hadn't tried to rouse her deliciously from her sleep. Tasneem walked over to the window. The night sky was mottled lavender and mauve, and the winds thrashed recklessly. Something pale flickered dully on the garden table, like a creature with a broken wing. She peered down and then realised what it was; the book she had bought from the market, blown open by the wind, rain splattering the pages like hard little stones, and just then she felt her heart dip like a moth falling away from a bright light. But the book would have to wait. It was not as though she could run into the garden, in the middle of a storm, in the silk lingerie she'd bought especially for this holiday. It was not the end of the world. Perhaps the pages would dry out, and even if not, she could easily buy another copy if she really wanted to, she could order one right now on her phone and have it waiting for her as soon as she got home, but still she felt for a moment a strange sensation not unlike the surprise of a small but painful sliver of a paper cut. 'He didn't think to bring it in?' she thought, that was all.

Tasneem looked up. She noticed how the sky here so high up in the hills looked frightening, how it seemed deeper and denser than back home. Somewhere behind the hills, she heard the echo of stray dogs barking, savage and fierce. She noticed how vast the space between each lonely star, far-apart distant planets vanishing behind the inky clouds and the endless dark.

No Phones at the Dinner Table

Jack Houston

it's a hippo and I've got the ears just about right I think and the roundness of its nose and the eyes and that's about it for a hippo because all I have to do now is draw the water around it and I hear step into the light shine so bright sometimes which is my WhatsApp alert and Dad says no phones at the dinner table and I didn't even remember he was on the sofa that sort of separates the TV from the dining table because I was concentrating on my hippo's left ear which just about matches the right ear now and I say but we're not even eating yet

Dad gets up and walks over to the kitchen the entire kitchen dining table TV area of our front room an L-shape and says it doesn't matter a rule's a rule and then says is that your WhatsApp? you should mute the notifications like I told you to but I won't because I need to know when my friends are saying the things they're saying and I sigh loud enough so Dad can hear me but not enough to get in any more trouble not that I am in trouble and I put the phone on the shelves squashed behind the dinner table and Dad stands in the kitchen and I can tell he's thinking something and maybe wants to say something but maybe doesn't know what because normally he wouldn't be that bothered by me using my phone at the dinner table even if and when we are actually eating dinner

Lorna! Dad calls into the rest of the flat which is only three more rooms and that's including the bathroom Lorna! Dad calls again and we wait in silence for Lorna to come Lorna! and Lorna shouts from our bedroom that she's coming Lorna always puts off coming to the table every dinner time and breakfast and lunch at the weekend not that Dad's even started cooking dinner and she's supposed to have a snack in between each meal even in school because the hospital said she has to but Lorna still somehow manages to hide food in her baggy jumper or I don't even know where and Dad doesn't like us saying the word anorexic because I think he thinks us not saying it will somehow make it not true and Dad smiles at me weakly in that way he used to when I was little and calls Lorna! again and it's not like I can blame her because everyone wants to be thin or at least thinner all my friends at school do and I suppose it's something I think about too and even Dad's a bit the same but Lorna's so thin the consultant at the hospital said it will start to affect her fertility and all sorts of other health things perhaps

my eldest sister Evie isn't here yet because she's at university up in Birmingham which is far away and is a good university I know this because Dad said it is though Dad was quite upset when she went there last year because Dad thought Evie could have got into

Cambridge or Oxford had she not messed around with Dan who got her pregnant and messed with her A levels not that Dad told me any of this I overheard him talking on the phone to Auntie Barbara his sister and I'm not supposed to know this because Dad didn't want me to find out because I'm only nearly thirteen but Auntie Barbara said something on the other end of the phone and I don't think Dad realised I was at the table drawing a picture of a horse quite a good horse I got the head and the way its back swept all the way down to its tail just right and its legs but I still wasn't happy with the hooves hippos are much easier because of all the water after I heard Dad on the phone to Auntie Barbara I asked Evie and she told me but also told me not to tell Dad that I knew and Harry Styles sings from my phone again on the shelf behind me but Dad looks at me with one of those don't even think about picking it up to check it looks as he calls out Lorna! again and Lorna comes in flustered pulling her jumper sleeves over her hands as if that will hide how skinny her hands are and she sits down and Dad sits down

and now both of them are sat here watching me draw a hippo

today Dad says we're going to be having clam pasta Dad's favourite like the one he and Mum had on holiday back when she was still here and he starts telling me and Lorna the story he's told us like a thousand times but we don't stop him of how the man in the swimming trunks came up the beach when they were staying near Rome and they were on the beach and the

57

man who was selling the clams tried to proposition Mum and he was holding his bucket of clams and trying to proposition Mum whilst also trying to sell his bucket of clams and Dad always tells us she didn't know where to put her eyes because the man's trunks were so small and so tight and he tells us of how she told him later she was worried he'd be upset because the man with the tiny trunks was so obviously trying it on with her but she didn't know where to put her eyes and Dad laughs again as he says he wasn't fussed because he knew Mum loved him and after they'd left the beach without the man in the tiny trunks or his clams they ordered the clam pasta at the restaurant they went to and it was the best thing they'd ever tasted and he's never quite been able to do the recipe as good

I can tell Lorna's been crying and it's probably Mark but she can't say anything about it to Dad because Dad doesn't know about Mark and she can't say anything to me because Dad's here in the room with us because Mark's old really old too old to be going out with someone who's only fifteen like Lorna is and it is a bit weird because I've seen him and he's got like a proper beard like how Dad did around the time of the clam incident in the photos we've got up on the shelves behind where my phone sings again but this time Dad doesn't give me the look because he's concentrating on Lorna and asking her if she's all right and Lorna just gets up and runs from the room and Dad goes after her and I am starting to get a bit hungry but I suppose I can wait a bit longer and will have to I suppose because Evie's not even here yet so I pick up my phone and check my messages and there's three from Sam asking what we think of Jamie and what she should do and then WHERE ARE YOU GUYS???!!!

none of us are supposed to be on Tinder because we're too young but it isn't difficult to enter your date of birth in so you're over eighteen that's what we do that's what Josie and Jessica and Sam did and that's what I did and most of the boys at Drayton and so is how to tell if a boy in your class or your year or maybe in one of the other years fancies you or not before you go and make a big fool of yourself by letting him know you fancy him and Sam wants to know if she should swipe right on Jamie and I'm a bit shocked and don't know what I should say because she knows I fancy Jamie and have done since we were in primary school and to say she fancies him now is to totally ignore the fact that she's heard me saying so many times about how much I fancy him and my feelings and to go and ask me if it's OK if she swipes right on him is not right I don't think

Lorna started not eating properly when she started at Drayton which was when she was my age which was nearly three years ago but we didn't notice at first and only found out how long it had been going on when Lorna told us at one of the family therapy sessions the eating disorder clinic made an appointment for because Dad didn't know what to do not that I know what to do because I'm the youngest one in the family and I can hear Lorna and Dad talking in our room and I wonder how much longer they're going to be in there because it's not like she's going to tell him why she's so upset he could be in there

59

forever and it could be forever until Dad starts cooking and I've finished the head and the eyes of my hippo and have even drawn one of those little birds that live on their backs I think there are little birds that live on the backs of hippos I'll have to check and I really am actually starting to feel quite hungry

step into the light shine so bright sometimes sings my phone again and I pick it up and turn the ringer off and I don't want to look at it or try making Sam feel any better over what is in fact a massive betrayal but I can't help but try and peer at the screen to see if it is her who's messaged the group again or one of the others and it is her and I bet she's already sent Jamie a picture of her boobs like Jess who said about sending a picture like that to Dean and then was worried Dean would show it to his friends but I don't think Dean did or would because Dean's actually quite nice but then I suppose people always seem nice until they aren't though it's not as if any of us have even got much in the way of boob though I suppose Jess does a bit more than me and Sam or Josie and in the light of the phone's screen I can see Dad's face in one of the photos that's been lit up by my phone screen just his face not anything else the photos lined up along the shelf in a sort of shrine I say sort of but it really is a shrine

what we try to do is reframe what has happened to us it's a sort of instinct the family therapist said even if that thing is terrible we will reframe it in an attempt to find some kind of peace but sometimes if the bad thing that happened is bad enough that's just not possible and all we can hope to do then is realise that it's OK for it to be bad the family therapist said and if we can do this then Lorna will be able to eat properly again not that the family therapist said that last bit about Lorna but I know that's what we were all thinking as Dad nodded and said mm-hmm

Mum died when I was three Lorna doesn't really remember all that much about her either because she was only six or something and it's not like I'm sad about it all that much because like I say I didn't really know her but I suppose she knew me and loved me and that's what Dad says he says she loved me loved us all very much but she had to go but the family therapist says that it's OK for me to be as upset as I like about it because if something is hard to process it's hard to process but I'm not sure I've processed anything

it's all I know

when Mum died Dad quit his job but we don't talk much about what happened then but we did have to sell the big house on Chisholm Drive only two roads away from here but we often walk past it on our way to and from school which Evie told me she remembers I'm not sure Lorna does but the flat we live in now is smaller and high on the fifth nearly the top floor of the block and has a really big window in the front room which is also the kitchen which catches the sun which makes the flat really warm even in winter and sometimes too hot in summer and Dad and Lorna come back in and Dad smiles at me sort of weakly and Lorna doesn't look at me

and now Dad's phone rings and he gets up and answers it which isn't fair if you ask me because how is he allowed to answer a phone if I'm not? and we hear him say hey and oh and no don't worry about it it's OK and I look at Lorna and she lifts her eyes to mine for just a second and then looks away and Dad says it really would be nice if you could try and make it and then he says oh no it's OK I quite understand and then he hangs up the phone and goes back over to the hob and looks at the kitchen as if that is going to tell him what to do and he doesn't say anything was that Melissa? I ask and he doesn't say anything so I say Dad?

it's a bit weird anyway Dad inviting his new girlfriend over on the night we're having our special clam pasta because we only have our special clam pasta on their anniversary his and Mum's anniversary which is why Evie is coming all the way from Birmingham and why Dad probably shouldn't have invited Melissa no matter how much he likes her and don't get me wrong I like her too she is actually quite nice and likes Dad even though he's quite old and going a bit bald and has a bit of a belly so could definitely do worse Melissa is obviously not Mum and never will be but even thinking this makes a funny kind of hollow feeling in my tummy because I don't even know if she is like Mum at all she looks a bit like her I can tell that from the photos but is her laugh the same? or her voice or the way Mum would have listened to me as if I was the only person in the world can she do that? and it's Dad and Mum's anniversary anyway and Evie's not here either

                                        Lorna shifts in her
seat and I think she's actually going to say something

                                                    but she
doesn't

                        Dad's still standing in front of the
hob like he's waiting for permission to start cooking and I hope he does soon because I am getting quite hungry and he sees me staring at him but instead of starting to make the food he gives me that weak smile of his that hasn't made me feel any better about anything since I was at least eight and turns and looks back at the hob so I look at Lorna who's just staring down and picking at one of her nails so I just start drawing another hippo in the pool a smaller one next to the bigger one and think that in the wild I guess a hippo would have a baby hippo with it are hippos mammals? we learnt about what makes a mammal that it's the milk they make and some other things but how does a baby hippo suckle with those big wide mouths and in all that water?

                        and Dad's phone rings
again and he picks it up and says hi yes and I can tell he's smiling even though he's got his back to us and he says that's great OK then we'll see you soon and he hangs up and says

to me and Lorna that was Evie she's at the station already she's getting in a cab I guess I should get the dinner on and Dad turns on the radio and takes the chopping board down from where it hangs on the back of the kitchen door and starts slicing into an onion

Dad always listens to classical music while he's cooking he says it relaxes him and it is sort of OK but not as good as the songs me and my friends sing in school in the playground or the songs we play at my after-school street-dance lessons and Dad starts to hum along to the music and there's a sizzling noise as he puts the chopped onion into the oil and the kitchen is filled with the smell and I look at Lorna but she's just staring at the tabletop probably planning how to get through dinner so I go back to my hippo and her baby and start drawing a few trees behind her but then I remember hippos live in the jungle and that they've got to be jungle trees and I wonder how a jungle tree might look different to the trees we have in the parks and along the streets around here

my phone vibrates and I know I could take it to me and Lorna's room or just the sofa but then I decide I don't want to get into discussion with Josie and Jessica and Sam about Jamie because I don't like talking about what he might look like naked and I think jungle trees have big leaves like the cheese plant we have in our front room and isn't that a funny name a cheese plant? makes me wonder what kind of things we could have named plants after like bread plant or sausage plant or clam pasta plant

Lorna fidgets in her chair and I bet she wants to get up and walk out again but Dad's probably already spoken to her about spending more time in here with the two of us even though I'm still drawing my hippo and her baby's jungle and Dad's now chopping the garlic so none of us are actually saying anything to each other not that I would know what to say to Lorna anymore not since she came into our room after a shower and I saw the marks on the tops of her legs near her hips deep red scratches but I knew they weren't just scratches from itching herself because she was bitten by a mosquito or something but that she'd been at herself with some scissors or something because we talked about it in our PSHE lesson with Ms Clarke who said she used to do it when she was younger and later Sam said her mum has scars on her arms and Dad says right and gets a tin of tomatoes from where we keep them on top of the fridge and pulls the ring pull open and pours it on top of the onions and garlic and says right again and then comes and sits down at the table and says ooh what are you drawing but then says the clams and gets back up again

and Dad tastes the sauce with the spoon he's using then stirs some more which is a bit gross because of germs and then grinds something salt or pepper into it tastes it again and says I'm putting the clams in now as if we need to know that and I look at Lorna and try to catch her eye as Dad takes the kettle that's just boiled and there's a whoosh as he pours the boiled water into the already heated pasta pan and says I'm putting the pasta on too the buzzer goes on the intercom and Dad turns off the radio and walks into the flat hallway and picks up the phone receiver thing that you talk through to speak to the person who called up to the flat from the street and I hear him say honey and you're here and where's your key fob? and says anyway you can tell us about it when you're up here and presses the buzzer and then turns to us and smiles but not one of his weak ones a proper one and then he walks towards the front door but stops and turns around and comes and sits back at the table with the two of us and I put the green-colour pencil I was doing the leaves of the jungle with down and Dad smiles at me again and I smile back and look at Lorna who also smiles

and in the quiet of the flat we can hear the lift murmuring up the lift shaft and then the click click click of the key-code door to the hallway outside and it creaking open and then our front door opening and there's Evie in her big coat and her hair piled on top of her head and saying hey how is everyone? and she puts down her bag and sighs and she looks funny different but I don't care and I get up from the table and leap the two to three steps across our small kitchen and wrap my arms around her and I've started crying and can feel Lorna hugging as well and she's started crying too and now Dad wraps all three of us in his big arms and Evie says hey it's OK it's OK

someone clears their throat from the doorway to the kitchen and we all look up from our group hug and Evie says oh yes this is Michael and there's Michael who's actually quite hot-looking in a normal sort of way and Dad wipes the tears from his eyes with one hand and offers the other for Michael to shake as Evie says we're not to worry as Michael's parents live not far from here well not too far and that they are going to stay with them while they're here and Dad asks if she's sure which is silly because we've only got the bigger bedroom between all three of us and Lorna and I have long piled Evie's bed with a load of our dirty washing and schoolwork and other bits and bobs and god knows what else and Dad smiles at Michael and says but you are eating with us right?

Chameleon
Rea Dennhardt

The first time an animal ever died in our house was the day Aunt arrived, wearing the same kind of khaki outfit Princess Di wore to clear landmines. She marched through our compound gates, placed a finger under my chin and wordlessly lifted my face, tilting it to one side, then the other. Mum introduced her, warily I think. On both their lips, smiles that weren't really smiles.

'You planted tea roses!' Aunt said, pointing to the scrubbiest corner of our garden and ignoring the lush climbing lilies flowering all over the high razor-wired walls that kept danger and Dar es Salaam out of our lives.

Taller than our mother, but with the same fair skin, Aunt spent her first day on the veranda, twirling slippery hair between her fingertips and telling us about life in England. Mum had her legs crossed and her head turned slightly away, only looked up when Aunt mentioned Dad. Sitting silently for hours, a toe twitching every now and then, Mum had the aura of an empty shell.

It was almost dark when Shabani called us to the kitchen. In his hands a dead, blue kitten. I surrendered completely, hands high and away from my body, in my chest the feeling of vacuum. Older, better at handling himself in these situations, Justice sank to the kitchen floor, eyes down and obedient. I shifted from foot to foot, bit my bottom lip, wished someone would remove this moment and wind us back seven days. Any version with Dad in it would be fine.

'Please sit, Leila.' Shabani's lips moved softly, his fingers air-crossed above my head. 'Her sin, her soul.' Slim and straight-backed, in a silk shirt and matching trousers, Shabani looked like the baddie in a Bruce Lee film. His gaze, sharp enough to halve us, crawled from child to child. I covered my face with my hands, slid my spine down the cold concrete wall and took my place on the floor of the world.

Shabani, Justice's father, our cook, and on most days my hero, paced in front of the unshuttered kitchen window. He'd ordered us by age, a sorry row of children and animals: Justice, my best friend; Brigadier, the dog; nine-year-old me; Mui, the cat. Our pets, bundled into tight balls, had their paws over their heads.

Shirt- and shoeless, my shorts bunching up below me, I waited for Shabani to find words. My fingers traced cracks and craters in the clay floor. I read the back of a twenty-kilo jute bag of Best Quality Basmati Rice. I counted the splatters of squashed mosquitoes. I watched cockroaches slip down the drain. My bum hurt.

'Search your minds . . .' whispered Shabani.

Searching my mind, I decided letting animals die without names was grievous, cruel. I started naming our victims in my head: Tiger, after the year, Toto, Tamtam, Toblerone for the shape of her ears . . . My breaths became smaller and sharper, punctuated by swallowed gasps. My insides shook. I was on kitten number six when Shabani squatted before me, dipped his head. His eyes, normally laughing, looked tired. He wiped a tear off my cheek and I realised that I was crying without even knowing.

'The washing machine,' I sobbed.

Justice groaned.

Shabani picked up the wet, violet-coloured cat to my left. He smelt of the Battenberg cake he'd made for our tea and I wanted to hug him, badly. I hugged myself instead.

'The cat is crying, Leila. She is missing her babies already.'

This was not true. Many kittens had come and gone. The cat never seemed to care. Still, kitten-deaths made the space around my heart hurt. I closed my eyes. It may have been Justice's idea to dye the cat-babies, but I'd found the tube behind the toolbox and oozed out the glistening indigo paste. We'd switched the machine on together. In this crime, we were equals. Shabani watched with questioning eyes.

'You wanted blue-fade kittens?'

'A matchy-matchy cat family,' I mumbled – a fragment of the truth. Justice also wanted to prove the theory that no self-respecting snake would eat anything blue. But the last reason, my main reason, my big one, I was too afraid to explain, even to myself. Just mentioning its existence terrified me. If I thought about it, or any of the other things I'd heard being said that day, I knew I'd never be the same again.

'Matching has no purpose on this planet.' Shabani's voice was considered and kind but the whites of his eyes were turning pink, and giving the impression they were about to explode all over our ignorance. 'Who hurts creatures that don't hurt anyone?'

I looked up, slow-blinked to take some blame. Mum was preoccupied with her sister, too broken to punish me.

71

But Shabani would show his son no mercy and flip-flops left painful welts. Justice kept his head down and I avoided looking at him; his beatings hurt more than my own feelings.

Having us line up against the wall, between our cat and dog and the tumbling spills of their dinners, was Shabani's idea of a shame-based punishment. As younger kids, we sat like this for our meals. He didn't know how much we still loved eating there. He also didn't know how relieved I was to see the cat crying over her dead kittens.

'*You* cannot punish *me*,' Justice said, eyeballing his father. '*I* do not sell animals to *eat*.'

The back of Shabani's head moved and I knew that his handsome face was scowling. He carried the cat to her cot. Out of his sight, the floor felt smoother and cooler. He knew that we knew he sold the last litter to the flute-playing loin-clothed man with the cobra in a basket. And, that he was paid double because they were voodoo white. Dad'd said we couldn't accuse the cobra of anything until we stopped eating meat ourselves. Dad had never even tasted an animal. Or a fish. Dad was still reliably lodged in my mind.

Aunt had come for his funeral. Around me, Aunt was unsmiling, but she was kind to Mum, fed her tea and toast and brushed her hair in the living room. From the kitchen floor, they looked like a tea party for matching dolls, Aunt sitting beside Mum, fanning both their faces with folded cardboard.

With Justice, Aunt was strange. She didn't say or do anything bad to him, sometimes the exact opposite, her voice too syrupy. It was just that near him, her face tensed a little, her gestures became stilted, her words more carefully considered. She stared at him with the expression of someone watching a fight and expecting, sooner rather than later, to be hit themselves.

The next day, with an aunt and without my dad, our routine changed. In between eating, we were no longer allowed to play the way we used to. I missed being lost to the ball, longed to run. The air became fragrant with the perfume of ladies sharing sympathy. I heard their words. I knew what they meant. I just couldn't match them to my life. And anyway, Dad said praising people was unfair when they weren't around to deny the miracles they were being accused of.

After the lady visitors, Mum looked tired, stared into space. I watched her from the living-room floor, with Cally, my new chameleon. Aunt spread herself over the sofa behind me and started pulling knots out of my hair with gentle fingers. Slow and careful, her tugs felt good. Until she started talking about taking us back to England. I jerked. Mum bit her lip. There was blood. I brought water but she wouldn't drink. Aunt told her to think about me. Mum said she was. Aunt told her to move on. Mum didn't answer.

'Then walk around Africa wearing a philosophy degree!' Aunt said, all teacher-like.

I stood completely still, until Aunt ushered me back to the floor, her glossy nails pointier than our parrots'. She ran her fingers through my hair for a little while.

'You're still young. You can start again.'

Mum's big toe twitched. I looked up, unsure who was being spoken to.

'And if you keep Leila out of the sun, she could pass. Some Magic Powder. Regular Fair and Lovely. Mediterranean. Mas o menos.'

Mum pinched her face into an angry ball, pressed it into our cat and screamed. Her reaction hurt, didn't contain enough of

73

the information I needed.

Aunt exhaled over my head. Her hot breath seemed to tear apart the air around me. I held the chameleon to my forehead, let her clamber over my head.

'Feral kids in a feral fucking house!' Aunt shot to her feet.

Mum opened her mouth, looked as if she was about to say something. I felt my spine straighten, waiting for whatever she was going to tell Aunt from me as well. But Mum stopped, the sentence in her head either erased or trapped behind the pain in her eyes.

I lifted Cally onto Aunt's *Designer Home*, took her outside. Aunt'd started 'doing' the house almost as soon as she'd entered it, because pretty-shaded places were easier to sell. To me, her pastels looked sludgy and unhappy.

'Strong White is bright, neutral, reflective,' said Aunt.

'Good taste is an artificial construct not a fact,' Mum said. I tugged her sleeve for an explanation, walked away without one.

On the Farrow & Ball boards tacked all over our walls, the facts were: I was String, Mum was Cord and Justice was Mahogany. In the two days since Aunt arrived, she'd gone from Cabbage to Cornish and her fingernails from Flamenco to Flamingo. Aunt was clear about not wanting a denim-shaded cat.

Shabani shaved Miu from Tokyo Blue to Kyoto Pink. Without her fur, she looked naked and a little rat-like, but towelled up thickly, she felt like she did before the kittens came. I nuzzled behind her ears. Kissed her. She meowed, glad, I think, to feel loved again.

'Do pink cats behave pinker?' I asked.

'You're treating her pinker,' said Justice.

'You're lucky she lets you kiss her already.' Shabani blew cat hair from Dad's electric razor. Switching it on again, he let it buzz long and low and steady. Brigadier stiffened his ears, looked around for Dad. I blinked back tears, inched towards Shabani.

That afternoon, quite suddenly, and for the first time since Dad died, Aunt demanded meat be cooked in our home. Mum was beside herself. In the tradition of my father's people, flesh couldn't be consumed for a year after a death in the family. Aunt called this third-world hooey. Mum called it respect. Everyone is superstitious, Dad said in my head.

'Zay's only six days gone,' Mum said.

'His religion isn't yours.'

'Animals were important to Zay . . .'

'But you're still the person you were born.'

'No one's born a religion,' Mum said through clenched teeth. 'No one's born anything except human.'

I put my hand in Mum's, squeezed slightly.

'Stop intellectualising grief.' Aunt began emptying kitchen cupboards.

'Then stop pretending to know.'

Aunt pretended not to hear.

'Aren't kittens enough? Do we need piglets and calves too?'

Mum stayed stubborn, clutched the doorframe high over my head as she spoke. Would not let dead flesh and bloodshed into the house. Aunt's face was all church-like when she said I was too small for my age. She said children needed protein to grow. That her body disagreed with our rice and vegetable diet. And that something was wrong in the heads of children who'd killed kittens before Battenberg cake yesterday.

Aunt's words wilted Mum slowly.

'They're upset,' she said eventually.

'Yeah?' Aunt raised an ambiguous eyebrow.

They compromised quickly after that: a mess-kitchen would be built in the yard and Shabani would buy a bird.

On the fourth day in the era of Aunt a live chicken was tied to the post between Justice's home and ours. We spent the morning feeding it funeral sweetmeats. I danced around it in an Arsenal shirt, the hem tucked into my shorts, peacock feathers stuck to my back with duct tape. Aunt stared down from her bedroom window, fanned herself with a paint library. I found her tight-lipped disgust quite motivating, practised full-body caterpillar moves around the bird. Dazed with dust, I grinned up at her. She turned away, shouted for Shabani.

In my head we became one that afternoon, the chicken and me, and I screamed when Shabani carried it towards the pot of boiling water. The bird recoiled in huge writhing motions when it felt the steam, made a sound too big for its body.

Plucking sounded like rocks being lifted off the earth after heavy rain, a sloppy sucking sound, not unlike a kiss. Justice and I sat at Shabani's feet, too shocked to speak. The dog joined us, salivating.

'Cage, Brigadier,' Mum shouted, draping the parrots' cages with torn bedsheets. I got the feeling she'd like to put us all in cages and cover us with dark cloth until both the chicken and the aunt had left our lives. Nothing this dramatic had ever happened in our house. Even Dad just woke up dead one morning and left under a sheet on a stretcher. A heart attack, the doctor said.

Momo, the grey parrot, kicked off the *Waltons* routine Dad'd taught her. My heart felt attacked. 'Goodnight Leila.

Goodnight Justice,' Momo said again and again, rubbing herself against the bars of the cage. Her words wound their way through the house and Ryder, the red parrot, made parroty noises in reply. He was a bad-tempered bird, started pecking Momo after she learnt to speak. For a while, Dad tried to figure out if Ryder was racist or sexist or just jealous, then concluded being nasty was bad enough and tried to release him. Only Ryder wouldn't fly away, kept looping back into the house, scared of freedom and facing everything he didn't already know and couldn't bear to see. In the end, Dad segregated them, said Ryder had the kind of brain that couldn't adjust to his changing position in the world, but that we still had a responsibility to stop him self-harming every time Momo spoke. I heard Mum throw pomegranate into Ryder's cage and curse Dad's no-pet-left-behind policy.

'The parrots won't hold the chicken against you,' Aunt said.

'Why are you always so sure?' Mum didn't believe in karma, but secretly worried it might exist.

I didn't want any chicken but Justice did. Aunt pinched my cheek encouragingly. With Justice, her hand seemed to think before touching. He pretended not to notice, but I felt the twinge. Yesterday too, during the Scrabble Aunt'd brought.

'You don't get the spirit of the game,' she kept saying, her tight smile winding itself tighter after each of Justice's wins.

'We agreed on any-lingual.' Mum sounded tired, didn't look up. 'Justice's Mandarin is just better than your Swahili. His Human too.'

Aunt blamed her migraine, pranced out as if she was the world's best thing.

Mum sucked her cheeks in a little. It made her face look hollow.

77

'She doesn't want to believe it's true,' Mum said. The look on her face was waiting, waiting.

Years later, at my aunt's funeral, her daughter told me Mum'd sent Aunt tagged photos for the rest of her life. *Justice going up to Cambridge* #SpiritOfTheGame. *Leila as Desdemona* #SpiritOfTheGame.

'I'm sorry,' I said, touching her arm and feeling awful.

'You should be,' she said, already walking away and killing a moment that could have been peaceful and tender.

It was early evening when Justice climbed onto the roof of his home, a two-room bungalow behind ours and a good place to tell ghost stories. About the same size as Brigadier's wire cage but made of sheet metal and sacking, it shook in the wind and made single raindrops sound torrential.

'The world looks flat from here,' he shouted.

I wanted to shin up too.

'After she leaves?' Mum tightened her grip on my shoulder, flicked her eyeballs in Aunt's direction. There were too many red veins.

'I am the tallest.' Justice backflipped, laughing as he landed. From upstairs Aunt filmed him for Myspace.

'Enough already,' Shabani shouted to his son as he poured cooking oil in the aluminium pot, tested the heat. On his outside table, pieces of chicken, beaten egg and breadcrumbs. My aunt called her recipe chicken nuggetinos and had given Shabani syllable by syllable instructions, proud in the way she was proud of everything from England. Watching her sister made Mum recoil.

'It's an illness,' she said. 'Your aunt needs to feel better than other people to feel good about herself.'

'Is she infectious?' I leaned into Mum.

Mum tapped her temple.

'Inherited from my mother, painful to cure.'

I squinted up at Aunt, watched her fan herself with the Farrow & Ball Z-fold. Felt sorry for this woman who may have to spend the rest of her days living in an unhappily ordered world of better and worse people.

'Enough already!' Louder this time. Shabani dropped a breadcrumb in the oil. There was the sizzle of frizzle-fry.

Pretending not to hear, Justice kept flipping, wiggly and loose. Not being seen wouldn't stop him feeling observed. Shabani's eyes could see around corners and like Dad, like Mum, like Brigadier, Shabani felt us long before he saw us.

Justice stiffened his body, concentration creasing his face. Aunt clapped. Brigadier started corkscrewing in high, tight circles inside his cage. Mad-dog spinning was how we knew Dad's car was almost home. Staring at Brigadier, her hand lost in her hair, Mum started breathing gaspily.

I joined Brigadier in his cage. Standing on two legs, front paws latched through wire, we stared at Justice together, tongues out, snouts squeezed. On the Farrow & Ball, Brigadier was Brinjal. Like Dad, Aunt'd said, which was why the dog loved Dad more than he loved us.

Justice must have planned to land in front of his father, arms wide, ta-dah. Instead he hit the pot of oil which hit the kerosene. A crackle. A snap. Too much light and fire to see. The yard smelt of charred flesh and burning hair. Mum screamed. There was terror in her face.

'This wouldn't have happened if your dad was here.' She wrapped Justice in wet towels. Shabani rushed the bundled body to the car, laid him on the back seat. Mum squeezed into the floor space behind the passenger seat. Shabani was driving before the door closed.

I crumpled onto the veranda steps, held my head in my hands. My heart felt everywhere at once. Behind me Aunt's steps were high-heeled and tripping. She wanted me to eat chicken-mushroom-cloud pie. I couldn't, but the cat did. Listening to the World Service, she scrubbed our kitchen for hours and hours with litres of blond Domestos. I heard her talking to herself.

'At every level,' she kept saying. 'This is wrong at every level.'

Her bleach burnt the inside of my throat but I stayed put. The night was stunned and starry.

When they brought Justice back from hospital, his eyes had aged. The burnt part of his body was covered in soft yellow bubbles. Sunshine Citron on the Farrow & Ball. He spent the night in my bed, his father on the floor beside him. The next morning some of Justice's skin had darkened to Chinese Emperor. Mother daubed him in a pink mixture that smelt of the earth.

'I am Calamine Pink.' Justice's face cracked like setting plaster.

'Please think about fun things.' Mum smiled for the first time since Dad died. I think she knew she was smiling, too. Looking after Justice suited her.

For the next week, our lives shrink-wrapped around Justice. We spent our days on the bedroom floor, playing with Cally.

'Do you think Cally feels green or just looks green?' I pushed a square called Cooking Apple into her hands, turned to Justice. After all, I was still String, but he'd become a shade-shifter with a tongue.

'I feel like me,' Justice whispered.

He watched me pass Cally squares I'd cut from the fashion magazines my aunt scattered around. Long legs, well-defined arms and flat faces, ordered by skin tone. The chameleon managed too easily. We moved on to clothing. She conquered neons. She smashed stripes. She overcame polka dots. I liked her best when she was purple and green and had one eye looking forward, the other back. Watching her adapt made me happy.

'What if we make her a colour we think is sad but inside she feels happy,' said Justice, his eyes wide. We mulled this tragedy until Mum said skin was just the waterproof membrane that held our insides together.

'Membrane?' Justice and I said in tandem. I think we twitched too.

'Like sticking plaster.' Her face looked happy, imagining, so we didn't tell her what Aunt'd said about matching membranes. 'In the future,' Mum said, 'we'll feel people's souls, not assume from appearance.'

In the present, having been inside the hospital mainly for Blacks, she wanted to get Justice skin medicine from the hospital mainly for Whites and needed to pay the doctor to write a child's prescription without either of us being there. We'd seen my father do things like this and showed her with the Monopoly money Aunt'd brought.

'Corruption will kill us,' Mum said, before learning the necessary sleight of hand in an afternoon. The special way to flat-palm and pass a banknote in a handshake. How to look away when the doctor smeared his palm across his chest and coughed. To act both innocent and pained.

I think Mum thought we were too young to know these things, wished we could unlearn them. But the next day, once she'd come back with the medicine, proud and smiling, we all knew she'd experienced something that would make her feel she belonged to the country we lived in. She looked stronger, for the first time since Dad died.

For the most part, Aunt stayed away from our patient. She beaded her wrists at the mall so her arms looked like sea-snakes. She ordered heaps of clothes from Alibaba for Mrs Doctor Roy. She planned to wear black to the funeral and didn't think I should wear white. I had an opinion on how I felt in the new black clothing, but not on how I looked. Aunt said looking was more important than feeling. Mum disagreed quietly. Aunt smiled. Later she took me to the side and told me about Ben Kingsley and Freddie Mercury. She suggested I try liking the things the English internet liked. I tried. The experience was faintly terrifying.

The day before the funeral, Aunt took me to the Quality Mall. Delicious and dazzling, it was where we'd gone for ice cream with Dad. Tutti-frutti for him. Always tutti-frutti. Double-dipped if we'd been good.

She flitted through racks of loose cotton outfits, the kind Mum wore, left them higgledy.

'She carries it off because she's beautiful,' Aunt said wistfully. 'Your mum could have had anyone . . . Someone . . .'

I swallowed, felt alone, outmatched by an aunt I couldn't ignore. Not knowing if she meant we weren't good enough for Mum, or simply weren't wanted without Dad, felt awful. I blinked back tears.

'Stop being such a sensitive sausage!' Aunt giggled,

walked off, her in front, me preferring not to have been one step behind, but not daring to pull up.

At the make-up counter, she made me close my eyes for a surprise, told me self-improvement was a good thing.

'Skin first.' She painted my face with her fingers. 'Always skin first. It's our largest organ, tells the world what we eat, how we live, who we are, where we came from, who we'll be. Skin tells us everything.' Her motions were short and feathery. The gloop felt like nothing I'd ever touched before, no substance I could identify. It smelt of sickness. I closed my eyes tighter, thought of Justice and his lotions of pink-yellow-browns. My face felt gooey and uncomfortable. My heart started thumping in my head. She shushed me, breathed on me heavily, mumbled something about symmetry and even cover.

'Your mother changed after she met your father –'

Inside, I felt a few lights go out. I didn't want to talk about my father with someone who disliked him. In my head I heard him, telling me to live up to my IQ. I told him I couldn't. I told him I was goose liver. He told me to be grit.

'Open your eyes and look up.' Aunt painted my lashes. They felt furry, clammy, clamped. Like the cat and her poor dead kittens.

'There was this other guy back then . . . English, really successful now. Really . . .' She picked up a pencil and coloured my eyebrows in a way that made them look surprised.

'Your mum thinks you'll hate people not dropping round unannounced all day long. Hate having to wear sparkly, high-heeled shoes.'

Creamy pink gashes appeared down my cheeks.

'Arsenal wear red,' I said. I don't know why.

'You'll get a good education. Learn things that matter.' She smiled, piled my hair high on my head and clipped it there. Her magic powder had lightened my skin two shades. It looked like my father's on the stretcher that morning, his body buffalo-stanced, colder than the floor we found him on. I think I missed Dad more in that moment than I'd ever missed him before and may ever miss him again.

Aunt stood back on her heels to admire her handicraft, kissed her bunched fingers. She turned the mirror towards herself, widened her eyes and sucked her cheeks in as she examined herself in front and side view. The lines around her eyes looked like knife cuts.

The smell of my own face disgusted me. I looked like someone I didn't know, someone in someone else's life. There was nothing wrong with the face except that I didn't want it to be mine. It felt like a face I couldn't breathe in.

'I think you'll love London.' Her smile didn't quite reach her eyes.

My heart felt cold. I wondered if this was how cosmetics made hearts feel. I wondered if this was how my aunt's heart felt, all day, every day, except maybe birthdays and Christmas.

I started scraping my face. I started screaming for Mum and Dad. Spotting panic in her bug-eyes, I screamed louder. Tears ran down my murky made-up face, looked dirty. Beside me, Aunt faded from Show-off Brown to Tired-old White. I felt fear twisting through the muscles of her arms when she grabbed my shoulders and shook and shook.

A policeman in Stiffkey Blue drove us home. Shabani crossed himself when he saw me. Mum screamed at Aunt with her eyes. I ran from the moving car, grabbed Mum's leg, prepared to never let go.

'She's a girl not a jungli.' Aunt shook her head.

'She's a little girl not a stencil.' Mum wiped the paint and the powder off with sloppy wet kisses and soft palms. 'And she'll never aspire to be you. Or anyone even almost like you.' The rest of what Mum said was unintelligible through tears – hers and mine. But Aunt seemed to understand. Her face lost that starched look of snotty unsurprise, started to quiver.

'Don't R-word me,' she shouted. 'Marrying someone brown doesn't make you better.'

'Sometimes you should know better than to say stupid things . . .' Mum kept talking, too fast and angry for me to follow. She talked and talked until everything that could be said, probably had been. Then she looked resigned – to herself, to me, to this situation none of us wanted to be in. Mainly, I think, she looked relieved, as if she'd just said something she really needed to say, something difficult that she hadn't quite understood herself, but would soon, hopefully, be able to explain.

Through her arms, I felt something in Mum give way, something soften inside. For the first time since the doctor came, all sad-faced and serious. For the first time since Aunt started talking about structured cultures with no malaria, no diarrhoea and no equator. For the first time since we'd killed the kittens instead of saving them by dying them the same colour as the cat so she'd love them and not leave them the way Aunt said. For the first time ever in front of Mum, words lined up in my head, formed on my tongue, fell out by themselves. And when she heard everything I'd never said before, Mum was crying too and shaking her head in a shocked way.

'The ball and chain of my husband's membrane?' Mum's hands were in my hair.

'Do I really hurt you, just by existing?' I finished, waited for her to explain, hoped she knew how to make the world feel better.

Mum looked as if she'd just received another great blow to the brain. Already on her knees, she sank to her heels. Her look of disbelief turned to indignation. Eventually, she stood to face Aunt without letting go of me.

'You need to make sure your daughter is prepared for the world the way it is.' Aunt touched her neck, looked away.

'Our world doesn't think like yours.'

There was anger and defiance in Aunt's eyes. I think she called Mum a traitor.

'You left.'

'Who?'

'Everything we stand for.'

Mum was shaking as she kissed the top of my head.

'Never my child.' It took her a while to get her next sentence out. Her tone was sad. 'Name me one person back home,' she said, 'who actually grew up happy.'

Shabani drove Aunt to the airport early next morning. It was a joyless goodbye. At home we sat around the leftovers of her memory: dusty, curled sandwiches, the bread, wet and leaky; ham, matt and ill-looking; oxidised apple; pale-pink tea roses. Justice deconstructed the squares of bread and meat into rows, built a mini-monument with chopsticks. Wearing our most pastel clothing, we fanned ourselves with paint libraries, and avoided talking about anything that might actually have to do with something. It only took ten minutes of acting Aunt to feel terrible.

'You know . . .' Mum was turning the Monopoly board into a Feelings Wheel. 'Your aunt. She just hasn't figured there are spectrums of light she can't see in.'

I nodded, tore up a square of Rosy-Row. Justice started on Snowball. Twelve ripping minutes later, there was an unchromatised volcano of confetti on the table between us.

Mum stretched out an arm, swept the pile into the box of things we'd burn with Dad that evening. Things that would remind him of us and our life together: mangos and magic tricks; ice cream and Ibsen; feathers and footballs; a puppy collar; baby teeth; lush climbing lilies; razor wire; tea roses that wouldn't grow.

Night Classes

Lucy Sweeney Byrne

'Are you coming, Hal?'

Laura was standing at the bottom of the stairs, watching her own fretful face in the mirror as she called up to their bedroom. Her face, she noticed, not for the first time, did not appear attractive when she opened her mouth wide; her chin sort of disappeared into her neck, made worse this evening by her scarf, already wound tight. She was getting hot, waiting in the hall.

'Hal?'

She was tempted to just leave, but also knew that this would cause more trouble later. If he didn't emerge soon, she would have to go up. She pictured it: climbing the stairs, him hearing the creak from the bed, the secret thrill he'd feel at having won, at having broken her. She saw herself opening the door, the lump of him, curled up under the covers with his back to her, or perhaps sitting on the edge, elbows on knees and hands together, looking down at his feet, waiting to be coaxed into conversation – waiting for her submission. Then what? She'd have to go to him, to kiss him, touch him, and let him slowly come round. She would then have to allow him to take off her gloves and scarf and coat, to prove that she was willing – no, *happy* – to stay there with him, because they loved each other and, to him, that would be the natural thing, the *right* thing, to do. Her mind running through it, she knew too that she would then have to submit to sex, to let him pull her down, and to appear to want it, so as to soften the hurt she'd caused him; to partake, at the very least, in the symbolic gesture of the two of them making love – making a baby.

Laura didn't want a baby. She'd told him so over dinner. She'd always said she wasn't sure, that she might never want one. And he'd said that was fine, he wasn't sure either, they could decide later. Now, they'd been married for four years, she was thirty-four, and Hal was thirty-six, and he'd said, over a low-fat, gluten-free, vegetarian lasagne (which he'd cooked), that he thought she should stop taking the pill – that they should start trying for a baby. She'd laughed into her plate before answering. His tone had been so earnest, so assertive, betraying it as a well-rehearsed statement. When she did respond, sipping from her wine before she spoke, trying to keep it light, hoping to move on from the topic quickly, he'd been so shocked, he'd literally stopped eating. He'd put down his knife and fork, and stared at her. Soon after, he'd quietly professed himself not hungry (Laura's plate was almost empty, while he'd barely touched a thing), and taken himself to bed.

'Fuck this,' she muttered, watching as her cheeks began to redden in the hall, feeling the sweat begin to bead across her back. She didn't want to have to unparcel herself, she wanted to get going, to step out into the fresh, sharp cold, to walk briskly and listen to the evening sounds and watch her exhalations plume in bursts of white before disappearing into the surrounding air. She pulled at the front of her scarf uncomfortably. Whenever she got remotely too hot, she became convinced she was going to faint, although she'd never yet fainted in her life. She felt light-headed, and sick in her stomach. Please come to the top of the stairs . . . Please, she thought. If you would just come to the top of the stairs, if you would just come meet me in the middle, I'll consider staying. If you meet me halfway, we can talk about it, we can find a way. She glanced from herself to the clock on the hall table – 19.48.

'Hal, honey, I'm going! It starts in ten minutes, I don't want to be late! . . . If you really don't want to come, that's fine, we can chat when I get home . . . Or tomorrow!'

She'd paid for the class upfront, had even called the guy running it, Master Moshi, to make sure it really would be suitable for beginners. From the name, and the fact that it was karate, she'd thought he'd be Asian, but actually he was Irish too, from Derry, his accent thick and untainted by Chicago.

'Aye yeah, it's suitable for everyone,' he'd said, 'and some of us usually go for a drink and a bit of a chat after, there's one o' those gammy Irish pubs on the corner there – I don't drink myself, but I go along for the craic . . . Sure, you can always come along and see how y'feel. Aye, your husband too, and is he Irish as well? Ah right, ah well sure, haha, the more the merrier . . . Yep, yep, sound, see ya Thursday!'

She knew nobody from home here. Her cousins had grown up here, and were all living in the suburbs. They had kids already, but whenever she spoke to them they seemed to just complain about them, and about their jobs, and talk about what they were binge-watching on Netflix. Their main issue with Laura was that, amongst their own friends and colleagues, they prided themselves on being Irish. This made them uneasy around her – she who didn't speak their so-called 'Gaelic' or attend Irish Fests or play fiddle or wear green T-shirts and *Guinness Is Good For You* baseball caps on Paddy's Day, but actually came from Ireland. They'd been close as kids, but all they had in common now was a penchant for heavy drinking, and that, she'd found, wasn't enough to carry a night out together, although it got them through family weddings and Easter relatively painlessly. All of the friends she'd made through Hal and work were American, or, well, there was one French woman, married to a Canadian, and a Brazilian guy, and people with one or both parents from other countries, but they seemed to measure their success (and, thus, their happiness) by their ability to 'be' American; to belong here, in Chicago, in the land of opportunity. They talked about baseball and Trump and popular TV shows even more than the natives did, almost as though trying to prove the validity of their own presence – like every outing was a test of their green card credentials. But they were all interesting, all lovely – so what was her problem with them? Hal often asked her, saying she'd been quiet, even that he'd caught her rolling her eyes once or twice. She'd never managed to put it into words, but she felt now that what she missed was maybe something to do with being around people who understood themselves to be situated far from the centre of the world. She missed the feeling that came from being on a small island, with no more significance on a global scale than a baby-toe nail on a body. Although Ireland had been stifling when she lived there, from here, she remembered it feeling safe, easy, funny. She was sure there'd been less pomp, less earnestness, less you-and-I-can-change-the-world-ness. Her evenings out with Hal and his friends always began and ended with sincere, heated discussions on women's issues and congressional elections, as well as (for the born-and-bred Chicagoans) the heavily contested origins of the American blues.

'OK, sweetie, I'm going now, OK?' She watched herself in the mirror, cocking her ear like a cartoon dog. Nothing.

Fuckity fuckity fuckit anyway, she thought. She made a point of pulling on her boots noisily, banging them around a bit and hooshing herself down onto the second step to tie them, her coat rustling with the activity. All the time, she was listening out for him. Nothing. No movement. He was holding firm. Her stomach constricted. She began to hum, a Bill Withers tune, knowing he'd also be straining to hear every little thing, wanting him to understand that, as far as she was concerned, this was not a cause for concern – she wanted him to believe that, to her, this was all easy, all casual. No big deal.

Laura's mother hadn't wanted her to marry Hal. She'd never said it explicitly, was never anything but courteous towards him, but Laura knew. Laura could tell. Even on their wedding day, back in Ireland, it had been as though her mother was going through the motions. Her father had bawled his eyes out, had given Hal a big bear hug the moment the ceremony was over, had kept going on and on to all the American relatives who'd come over about how happy he was for 'my beautiful little girl', how Hal was 'such a gentleman, such a good fella', and how they 'couldn't be happier' to have him in the family. He'd called them 'the Yanks' and had bought them all pints of Guinness, which naturally they'd adored. Hal's younger cousins from Milwaukee had even asked to be photographed with him, had put little videos of him pretending to do a jig, elbows out and eyes half closed, on their TikToks: 'Irish Dad At Wedding OMG!!'

But maybe he'd known too, about her mother, and was overcompensating, Laura thought now. Her mother had acted properly, had worn navy-blue shoes and a duck-egg-blue dress, with matching short jacket and hat, had gotten her hair done, worn lipstick and her best pearls, had shaken hands and made conversation and smiled for the photos, but that was it. There had been a wall, a barrier, built up of all the unspoken things: her dreams for what Laura would become, an independent woman, travelling the world, an artist, all the things she herself would've liked to be, had she not fallen pregnant at nineteen; now dashed. Laura would become a lawyer's wife in Chicago. A lawyer who made supposedly tongue-in-cheek jokes about leprechauns, who talked openly and with relish about house prices and income thresholds and timely investments, and who'd teared up while reciting 'Scaffolding' by Seamus Heaney at the engagement party (seemingly the only Heaney poem he could find that fitted the occasion, although in truth it didn't). Laura's mind flinched at the memory.

She secretly wished (again, not for the first time) that her mother was here right now, to call bullshit. Without her mother's guidance, Laura found it very difficult, with Hal, to call bullshit. She couldn't even tell, now, whether there was any bullshit to call. Was his behaviour completely justified?

Whenever Laura thought he was being unfair, or petulant, or mean, he was able to explain to her, slowly and patiently, how she was wrong. How in fact she was the one being stubborn, or pig-headed, or cruel. He had shown her, more than once, how she was weaponising their respective genders against him, making it seem as though he was playing

94

the role of the 'unkind husband', when really all he ever wanted was to be with her and get along with her and live their lives happily ever after. She wasn't stupid; she knew about gaslighting, about bullying within a relationship, and emotional manipulation. The difference was that Hal really did only want what he felt was best for the both of them – he sincerely wanted to be with her, to spend his entire life with her, and for each of them to be given the opportunity to better themselves as well as the other. He took her criticisms seriously, had stopped whistling around the house when she'd asked him to, had worked on his technique, when giving head. He'd even bought an e-book about it, written by some legendary Peruvian-American sex therapist with a PhD and an all-women podcast. Yet, in spite of all this dedication, all of this 'constructive growth', and even though he'd never said it directly, Laura had come to understand from their marriage that she was an exceptionally cold person. Cold, and quite selfish. And even with these flaws, Hal loved her. So maybe he was right, to be so upset? And maybe, as she'd always suspected, there was something seriously wrong with her, for not wanting children.

This question, openly thought, made Laura feel for a moment as though she might actually throw up. Laces tied, she sat still on the stairs, doubled over into her thick coat, considering. Had she misled him, about having kids? Was it a given, that she was eventually supposed to want them? Were all women supposed, in the end, to want them? But she didn't. She pictured one, a little mewling baby; getting up in the night to feed it, never rid of it, always tied to it, never able to just get up and go and walk out, or to take a train somewhere, or be free. Not that she did that much anyway, took trains to places unexpectedly (in fact, she never did), but with a baby, the option would be gone – gone *for ever*. Laura treasured the notion of her freedom, even if she never actually made any use of it. It was like a gemstone, hidden away in her pocket, unseen, but there for her to touch, to stroke, whenever she felt like it.

Maybe this was just more proof of her selfishness, this need to keep her options open. She had married Hal, but that, she knew deep down, was less *definitely* permanent than a baby. She could, if she absolutely had to, leave a husband, but she wouldn't be able to leave a baby. Not that she intended to leave Hal. Laura believed in marriage, believed in making it work. Her parents had been through terrible times – her father's drinking, the infidelities, the roaring fights – but they'd always come through. And now they were about as happy as a couple their age could be, she reckoned. They'd be lost without one another, at least. And that was something.

Part of the attraction, for Laura, had been this sense of permanence, and the introduction of boundaries. Of limits. She had been brought up on a bright, white plateau of endless opportunities and horizons. All her life, her mother had insisted that she could be anyone, do anything, go anywhere. It had become a strange and, eventually, a crippling burden – all that wide-open hope, poured into her, by her mother, her culture, her position as middle-class, intelligent, healthy, capable. A husband, a particular place to live, a commitment of some kind, anchored Laura. It provided her with an outline, a life-shape, *within* which she had hoped she would be, if anything, more free.

Still, in spite of all the warnings about how difficult marriage is, offered by women's magazines and most of

Laura's unhappy aunties, it had proved even more challenging than she'd imagined. Knowing it to be reversible, knowing herself to still hold the *possibility* of total freedom, had helped her to cope with the tight strictures of her days. Cleaning, grocery shopping, keeping fit, keeping busy, seeing people, not to mention her work as an assistant to one of Chicago's top corporate photographers – all of it was OK because, ultimately, if she needed to, she could up and leave. When she thought this logic through to its end, it made her feel uncomfortable. Maybe she had never really committed fully to her marriage? Maybe the coldness Hal accused her of was actually something clinical, or a sign of something deeper, something unfixable. Probably, she thought, squeezing closed her eyes for a moment.

Laura untied her boots, and tied them again, tighter. Then she stood. What to do? She saw herself in the mirror, and caught, before she could adjust it, her worried, tired expression. She spent an inordinate amount of time reminding herself to unfurrow her brow, and was always unconsciously running her fingers between her eyebrows, to smooth out the deep groove that was forming. Recently, in the evenings, watching movies with Hal, she'd found herself absently scrolling through her phone, researching options for filler treatments, and Botox costs.

Catching herself, she looked, in that moment, older – finally looked her age, perhaps. Even with her incoming wrinkles, people still told her she looked young. Most guessed her to be somewhere between twenty-four and twenty-six. Her skin had always been clear and firm, like her mother's. But now she was thirty-four. *Thirty-four*. How had that happened?

They'd started dating when she was twenty-eight. At

that point, she'd had a string of crappy boyfriends, her photography was going nowhere, and she was living at home. In spite of all those gaping opportunities, those hand-wringing expectations, she was, somehow, sinking into failure. And then along came Hal. A Tinder date, in Dublin for the night. Why not? she'd thought, sitting in the lunch room of the office where she'd been temping. Wealthy, charming, American. It'd be an experience, at the very least. He'd picked up the 'check', then the next morning, offered to extend his stay another week. 'Why don't we just see where this goes? Give it a chance?' he'd said, staring into her eyes and touching her hair as they lay in the hotel bed. His eyes were big and blue and lined with thick black lashes. It was as though he was playing a part in a film, but it was a film she kind of liked, in spite of herself. He was so shamelessly *Hollywood*, with his white teeth and expensive-looking plain T-shirts and cheesy texts – 'hey Laura, I just want you to know that you are one in a million' – it was ridiculous, but also refreshing. He fucked her every which way, but insisted, after the first drunken night, that they always be face to face when one or the other of them came. He wanted them to come together, and felt so strongly about it, about what it would mean for them, for their 'fledgling love', that she started faking, just to please him. The first time he believed they'd come together, staring at one another, his eyes had welled up with emotion. Then he'd buried his face in her hair, pretending he didn't want her to see how moved he was. It was sweet, she'd thought, stroking his back – romantic. A little ridiculous, but definitely romantic. The guy she'd been with before that had usually come on her back, and then left soon after.

Whatever else Hal had been, he was, she told herself

again, staring into the mirror, without question, an enormous improvement.

He'd been the one to suggest she move in with him, just three months later, after she'd had yet another fight with her mother. 'You'd like Chicago. It's too hot, then it's too cold, and the whole time it's *super* violent – good for photos, right?' he'd said laughing over Skype. She'd been to Chicago many times as a child, had gone with her parents to visit their family there, but Hal had always spoken to her as though she hadn't. He just blocked that fact out. Chicago was his to give to her. He kept saying he couldn't wait to show her around 'the *Windy City*!' He told her he'd take her out on the town, introduce her to everyone, maybe even throw a party. She'd told herself that this too was charming. She'd moved over immediately, booking the flights before she had time to think herself out of it.

And he'd done it all, and more. His apartment then had been beautiful, as was this house, which they'd bought a year later (with his family money, although he'd insisted on putting it in both of their names). He'd encouraged her to decorate it however she liked, to buy all new furniture, anything. She'd never been especially interested in interior design, but was touched by his faith, and threw herself into it. They'd painted the walls together, in the colours she'd carefully chosen. Pale, blue, mossy green, ox-blood red. Every time they opened a new pot for a new room, he marvelled, 'Wow! Oh my God, it's beautiful, so beautiful baby, what a great choice!'

He was invariably attentive, exceptionally kind. When she'd first arrived, and went for all those job interviews at magazines, or tried to pimp out her photographs freelance to newspapers, he'd supported her, believed in her, cooked comforting and nutritious meals for her. Whenever she was upset, or had bad period cramps, he ran foamy, scented baths for her. He bought her lots of little gifts, perfumes and lingerie, but he respected her opinions too, listened to her, watched the films and read the books she recommended, so that they could talk about them later. 'This Wuthering Heights, it's crazy, holy crap!!! Loving it, xxxxx' he'd texted her from his morning commuter train. He wanted to devour everything she could offer him, and told her that he wanted to give her back all he had in return. He taught her, without ever acknowledging it overtly, that this was how love worked – a sharing of what you had.

Usually, a night class like this would be more his thing than hers – she'd always hated group activities, until he'd shown her she needed to lighten up. 'Not everyone's an idiot, Laura. You gotta give other human beings a chance, y'know?' And although, mostly, they did prove to be idiots, he was right – some were OK. And it was nice to be amongst them, regardless, even if only to feel smug and superior at times. Hal had taught her the importance of regular human contact for maintaining her mood. Besides anything else, the busyness meant she had less time to overthink, and thus to be anxious, or to wallow. Now, she did a pottery class on Monday evenings, a knitting class every second Tuesday, Zumba on Fridays and spinning on Saturday mornings, while he went to the gym on Mondays and Tuesdays, did yoga on Wednesday mornings before work and played baseball with friends in a local league most Sundays in the season. And, right now, this very moment, they were *both* supposed to be starting eight weeks of Thursday-night karate, with the option to extend.

'Sweetheart?'

With tension sending electric currents up her hot, sticky back, she waited for a response. Nothing. Her face looked especially aged under the hall light, she decided; even her blond hair looked ashy and grey. The more she stared at herself, the less her face looked like her own. She suddenly wished she had her camera to hand, to capture this moment.

Then she remembered that she used to do this all the time – take self-portraits. Herself at her worst, her most raw, when she'd been crying in her room for days, or when she was agonisingly hungover. She'd created an anti-Instagram account, called herself Liera O'Deatherty, and filled it with the most awful, revoltingly honest selfies; of pus-filled, yellow spots on her face, or her own boozy puke in the loo, or strange, hard-to-discern images of the rolls of fat on her belly when she leaned forward, taken so close up that they looked like the patterns made by the tide on a pink sandy beach or an unfinished Georgia O'Keeffe landscape.

How had she forgotten about that? she wondered. And why had she done it? She remembered she'd thought it was artistic, made some sort of artistic statement. Something about lies, narratives, lived truth. All the usual I'm-in-my-twenties-and-I-still-have-ideals artistic notions, no doubt. The thought made her strangely sad. So sad that, for a moment, she felt like crying. Liera O'Deatherty had only had around thirty-seven followers, and most of those were bots, or her relatives. And yet, she felt, remembering it so sharply – the very fact of remembering at all, highlighting to her all of the things about her younger self she might still be forgetting, the things she might forever, now, forget – as though she had lost something, something irrevocable. It came to her, however fleetingly, as an acute and poignant grief.

Thinking about it now, standing silently in the hallway of her marital home, in America, so far away from that place, from that time, miles and miles of land and ocean and years already spent, Laura heard without registering the sound of someone walking by on the pavement outside, and wheels, pushing something, a buggy maybe. A car passed, then another. Someone nearby was trying to parallel park – she could hear the engine shifting gears back and forth, the squeak of tyre against kerb. In the distance, a siren. The house, silent too, hummed. Was this how she was going to live the rest of her life? Was this how she'd see it out? She glanced at the clock – 19.53.

'Right!' she said, sighing loudly.

'Cunting fucking fuck this,' she muttered, frustrated, but also trying to pump herself up, to convert her grief and fear and weariness into rage, the way she'd often seen her father do, when her mother had upset him. He'd never been one to cry, he'd get angry. It was the same with her mother, actually, although her anger had been silent, delicate, the black-hole anger of quietly closed doors and pursed lips, rather than that helpless raging outward; her mother's had, of course, invariably proved more deadly.

'Fucking selfish cunty pussy *dick*,' she said, a little louder this time, shoving away the rising guilt, picking up her backpack, retrieving her keys from the bowl. Now, decision made, rage growing freely, expanding out from her stomach like a mushroom cloud unfurling in slow motion, she moved swiftly, forcefully, keen to get out, to get free, out of that toxic heavy lovesick air as quickly as she could. She jerked open the front door, felt the whoosh of cold hit her hot cheeks, and smiled.

'Fucking wanking cunty cockface *bastard*!' she announced into the night.

'Bye then!' she called over her shoulder, almost giddy now, almost laughing in the surging and delightful hate she was allowing herself to feel for him, for this, for everything. Fuck the house, fuck the street, fuck the night, fuck the air, fuck Chicago, fuck everything that this living is turning out to be! Fuck it all, and then fuck it again for good measure! Leave no stone unfucked!

She would go to the night class, fuck it, why not? She'd work up a sweat, chat to people, chat the ear off them, be her most charming fuckity-fuckit self, and then she'd go out and get wasted, totally fucking wasted, like she hadn't been for years! Through her mind flashed an image of Hal's loving face – his face from the early days, that seemed always to be mouthing the words 'I adore you' in her memory – and in that moment, for the first time, she felt absolutely no love for him. 'Fuck him!' she almost shouted, smiling. She felt, just then, how school shooters must feel – elated on pain, *high* on hate. She stepped outside. She may have heard something from upstairs, some movement, a light step perhaps, or the creaking of a door, but she chose not to register. Ah, that cold, sharp air! The same air swirling all the way from here, this very moment, all across the world – across deserts, seas, cities, fields, rivers, forests, fishing villages, sandy beaches and glacial plains, on and on for ever; across all the bodies, the eyes and breasts and smalls of backs, the knees and shoulders and cocks and pussies of the world, the sweat-slicked skins and soft-to-the-touch lips, and they were all hers, too, if she wanted them. She was still young, could still be free, and she discovered in this moment that she would be, soon, again – she could fucking *feel* it.

The Bhootham in the Mango Tree

Rajasree Variyar

'There's a bhootham in that mango tree,' my father says.

My eyes follow his outstretched finger to where it levels accusingly at a grand, leafy specimen of the bearer of my favourite fruit. The tree stands proud in a field of long grass that holds the ominous potential of lurking cobras.

'Is it there now?' I ask.

Acha beckons me closer.

'She's there,' he says, pointing again, and I squint. Just beyond the shade of the balcony, the heat of the midday sun creates a distinct shimmer above the Keralan soil.

The mango tree is immune from the sweat I can feel trickling between my breasts. It protrudes from the edge of the tangled jungle that borders the field, currently empty of grazing cows. Its only inhabitant – that I can spot with my two mortal eyes – is a coal-black bird, glossy in the light, grooming its feathers. I watch its wicked beak bobbing up and down beneath its left wing.

'Do you mean the crow, Acha?'

Other than the odd word that works best in Malayalam – the *Achas* and *bhoothams* of our conversation – we're speaking in English. I'm not complaining. I love my mother tongue, the soft syllables of the word for 'father' sounding like a caress. But my Malayalam's terrible. I can understand it, but I have the vocabulary of a seven-year-old. To comprehend my mother tongue but speak it like a child – it's a cruel oxymoron.

He looks at me as though I'm crazy. I know the look – people throw it at Acha all the time, although thankfully he never catches it.

'Don't be silly,' he says. 'There, sitting in the tree. All dressed in white.' The frown creasing his brow eases, receding like the tide from the shore, and his eyes drift away. They widen, with a child's wonder. He's remembering, although these days his memories are a swirl of fact and fiction, mingled and kaleidoscopic, like a rainbow Madeira cake.

'That's where I saw her first,' he says. His gaze wanders back to the tree. 'She had hair like yours, thick and long. But she wasn't sitting in the tree. She was walking under it, towards me. Singing.'

I watch him carefully. He seems calm. I imagine his mind as a placid valley in summer. The days when the calm rolls away before a raging storm of delusion and paranoia never seem far off. I hope this peace will last, just for one more week, until we're safely back in London.

'Do you know what a bhootham is?' Acha says. He always starts a story with a question. He's holding my hand. His long, elegant fingers would have been amazing over the keys of a piano. Until the first storm, they'd been tapping at computer keys, speaking languages like Ruby and Python. Sometimes Acha's stories are about computer code, about it spiralling around him or telling him secrets, and I'm lucky if I understand one word in three.

But he's not talking about that now. Bhootham. I used to

hate it when he tested my knowledge like this, back before he began to change. Now I'm glad. I wrinkle my nose and try to think through what I learnt from the comics he used to buy me at the railway station when we travelled by Indian sleeper train. 'Some sort of demon or banshee?'

'Ghost,' he says. 'They're chained to this world by tragedy. That's what a bhootham is, a disturbed, searching soul, unable to escape its desire to remain here.'

Creepy. The words seem at odds with the sunshine outside, the lapis lazuli sky, the moist smell of soil and vegetation. I look at Acha, his face so like my own other than a slightly squarer jaw. His cheeks seem thinner than ever, making his dark eyes, framed with lashes almost as thick and long as mine, look huge. The question slips from my mouth almost reluctantly. 'Where did your bhootham come from?'

'Right here,' he says. 'A long time ago. She speaks to me sometimes. Sometimes she sings.'

I stay silent, waiting, but it seems he's run out of words for now. Instead, he shivers, from a chill that can only be imagined in this heat. I lean forward in my plastic chair, sticky with the sweat seeping through my salwar trousers.

'Are you OK, Acha?' I ask.

He blinks and his head jerks, as though he's forgotten I'm there. Maybe he has. He moves in and out of worlds in fits and starts, as though he's living many lives in one. But then his gaze meets mine and he smiles.

'Do you smell that? It's lunchtime.'

We've been in Thrissur almost a week now. At first, it was good to be away from uni – Warwick is miserably grim at this time of year – and the looming threat of graduate programme applications. Thrissur is apparently some beautiful ancient Keralan city, complete with Bronze Age stone temples and medieval palaces. My experience of it is patchy Wi-Fi and having to visit swarms of relatives. Most pay as little attention to Acha and me as possible, as though we're carrying an embarrassing contagious disease. My patience for the whole thing is fraying. I'm thinking enviously of my mother, who refused to come.

Acha is right. It is lunchtime. The dining room is cool and dim, just like most of the chambers and crevices and niches in this centuries-old house. It used to lodge several generations of the family, all living together in a mad, chaotic, loving tangle. Now, my grandfather lives here alone except for a few loyal house staff and a steady stream of relatives paying respectful social calls. The thick stone walls and small windows keep the heat at bay. The rooms smell of incense, old wood and must.

My grandfather sits at the head of the table, my aunt, uncle and cousin, down from their home in Bangalore, arrayed around him like retainers. He's a doctor, respected and revered in the town for years, and each year has added another layer of lacquer to his character. I call him Achacha – another beautiful word, a susurration, a soft caress. Acha's Acha. He's not a soft caress. He views his patients as puzzles. He views his younger son as an incomprehensible mistake.

Acha and I are seated at the end, the hangers-on, listening to a seamless mix of English and Malayalam conversation. My cousin Sanjana is on my left. She leans towards me.

'How's your acha going?' she whispers. They all refer to him like that, 'your acha', as though he's not their uncle, or their younger brother, or their son. They don't want to be reminded they're that close to him.

'He's great,' I say through a mouthful of fried fish and warm chapatti.

Sanjana hesitates. She wears full make-up and her hair's streaked with red-brown highlights. I remember the days when we used to play tag in the long grass of the fields, heedless of death by snakebite, and eat chocolate Nesquik powder out of the tin in the pantry, and paint each other's nails.

'You spend a lot of time with him,' she says. 'What do you talk about?'

'Of course I do,' I say. 'He's my father, not a stranger with a coke habit. We've got plenty to talk about.' I smile to take the sting out of my words, although I only half mean it. She can't be expected to understand, I tell myself.

The tops of her coffee-coloured cheekbones have turned a deep mahogany. She turns back to the main conversation.

Acha says to me, as though we had never paused to come inside, 'This bhootham used to be a young woman. A house maid.'

I nod in encouragement.

'She had a lovely voice. She'd sing as she swept the floors with the coconut-palm broom. At night, she sang to the children of the house and her voice was like silk.'

'Don't forget to eat, Acha,' I say.

At the other end of the table, my aunt calls Narendra Modi a hard-line Hindu and a dictator-in-training. I resist the urge to applaud. A hush falls over us. All eyes are on my grandfather. He waits, although he already has our attention. 'Any man,' he says, 'who upholds and fights for Hindu values must be respected.' My aunt looks like a chastened but defiant schoolkid. 'For centuries the Hindus have been downtrodden and now it's our time to be –'

'She's hiding,' Acha says suddenly. He's louder than he has been for a while. His voice cuts through my grandfather's voice, startling him into silence. Everyone turns to stare at him. He doesn't seem to notice. Instead, he's looking past us towards the kitchen, as though he can see something we can't. 'Just like she used to hide in there. She doesn't want to face us all.'

I put my hand over his. His fingers fold into a fist beneath my palm, and he leans forward as though he's about to stand.

'It's OK, Acha,' I say. 'There's nobody there. I'm here.' Stay calm when he's not, I've learned. Calm's contagious.

The family are lowering their gazes from us, then turning away. Murmurs are starting up, soft as the hum of bees. My grandfather is still silent. He's staring at Acha, his upper lip curled.

'We should find her,' Acha says, still too loudly. 'She's hungry, and alone. Out by the mango tree.' He's still fixated on something visible only to him, his eyes bulging, but he's settling back into his chair.

My uncle looks concerned. His mouth opens, but before he can say anything my grandfather speaks. 'It's rude to interrupt, Arun,' he says, his voice quiet. 'You never could understand that, could you? Even before you lost your mind and spoke nonsense.'

'He can't help it, Achacha,' I say. 'And it's not nonsense. He just sees the world differently.' I want to scream at him, Screw you, you're a doctor, shouldn't you know?

My uncle jumps into the gap. 'Hey, Arun, guess what's showing at the Ganam theatre? They've remastered

Manichitrathazhu. Arun? Do you remember watching that, years ago?'

Acha's gaze moves back to us, seems to focus finally on his brother. I feel his fingers relaxing.

'We can go tonight,' my uncle says. 'Who's in?'

Sanjana's all enthusiastic agreement and grudging gratitude sweeps through me. I muster a smile for her as the conversation steamrollers on.

I've lost my appetite. So, it seems, has my grandfather. He sits back in his chair, his eyes flicking over each of us so deliberately it's clearly no accident he never once looks at Acha.

In the end, we all go to the cinema, everyone but my grandfather. I haven't seen a Malayalam movie in years. They ooze with drama so thick and sticky you feel as though there's a spiderweb wrapping around you, trapping you in your seat. But Acha's more animated than I've seen him in a while.

The movie's about a young couple who buy an ancestral house that looks like the one we're currently staying in. The house is haunted, by a nineteenth-century dancer forced to become a concubine and then murdered in a jealous rage. We watch the young wife become possessed by the dancer's vengeful spirit – her bhootham. Despite the music, complete with piercing soprano voices and pulsing colours, I can hear my uncle snoring beside me.

The movie stops halfway through. The lights beam on, blinding me, and I'm confused until I remember the unique phenomenon of the Indian movie interval. Sanjana turns to me, grinning.

'How great is –' Her eyes move past me, past my sleep-dazed uncle. 'Where's your acha?'

The seat between my uncle and the aisle is empty.

He's left his glasses behind.

Thrissur at night is more chaotic than it is by day. The tumult has become a thousand moving points of light breaking the darkness. Glaring headlights, flickering lamps, multi-tiered, hanging outside temples, harsh fluorescence spilling from the always open streetside shops. My chest is tight with lack of air as I sit in the back of my uncle's Toyota. The window's open, the air as heavy as a moist towel. The cloying pungency of vegetables on the verge of rot settles in the back of my throat. It mixes with the smell from the roadside restaurants, curries and dosas and frying samosas. The traffic's forcing us to move so slowly I'm struggling not to cry. Surely a car should be travelling faster than a meandering man on foot. Instead, we're waiting as a cow takes its easy, oblivious time crossing the road.

We've assumed that he's walked down the main road alongside the cinema. The alternative's horrifying – that he's wandered blindly into a tangle of streets and alleyways, to get hopelessly lost, to run into people who might beat him for his wallet or his strangeness. The others have taken a cab home, in case he heads that way.

The cow moves off and so, finally, do we. I scan the faces flashing past us, watching for Acha's hunch-shouldered walk, my eyes searching for his thin arms and the pastel green of his shirt.

We drive ten minutes down the road, further than he could walk in an hour.

Nothing.

Turning back, we hurtle as fast as we dare to the cinema complex. The car weaves through the maze of streets around it, dodging stray dogs and street vendors packing away for the night. We get stuck behind a random procession of priests and devotees hefting a golden deity above their shoulders. As they sing, the smell of jasmine and marigold seeps through the air-conditioning vents.

No sign.

My uncle suggests we head back to the house. His voice is tight. Eventually, he says, when whatever spell's beckoned him out of the cinema fades, Acha will head home.

I nod, wanting desperately to believe it.

I run up the front steps into the house. 'Did you find him?' Sanjana and I ask at the same time, answering each other's question.

'I'll go out again now,' my uncle says.

My grandfather sighs and raises a hand to his head. '*Kashtakaalam*,' he says. Hard times. 'He'll wander back eventually.' And he mutters, in what his old ears hear as an undertone, 'No bad thing if he doesn't.'

I can't be here anymore.

'Maya,' someone calls as I run out of the room and keep running, down the steps and across the drive.

At the back of the house is an artificial lake, an ancient man-made pool. Time-worn stone steps lead down into the cool depths. This is where my father bathed at five in the morning and six in the evening, every day, for the first seventeen years of his life.

A stone bench stands in front of the pool. I sit down, the granite still warm from the day's sun, and look out over the water.

113

Long minutes pass before my breathing slows and I can think again. I don't want to think again. I want to lie down and sleep and wake up to find my father standing over me, smiling, like he used to do when I fell asleep stargazing on the trampoline at home.

I can't just sit here. I'll walk around, willing him back. I'll be a beacon, guiding him.

The night's a sheet of darkness rippled with moonlight. It's starting to rain, thick, solid drops that splatter like water balloons in the dirt. Mosquitoes keep me company as I carry on beyond the back of the house.

I turn the corner.

There's a figure under the mango tree.

For a moment, I think someone's abandoned a statue there, kneeling, hunched. But then it moves, straightens, its head turning up towards the branches, and the faint light turns the pastel green of its shirt even paler.

I'm running.

My sandals slap the ground, drowning out the cicadas, but he doesn't seem to notice. I stop inches from him, breathless with relief. 'Acha? Acha, where have you been? What are you doing here?'

He continues to stare into the tree, milky light leaking through the leaves and dappling his face. 'She keeps calling me,' he says. I wonder if he knows I'm here, but then he looks at me. Rain is dripping from his hair and down his face. He seems as tired as an ill child, the bags under his eyes ugly as bruises, and even though he's gazing at me, I'm not sure if he's seeing me.

I feel terribly, angrily alone.

'Acha, we've been searching for you. I've been so worried.

114

How did you get back?'

His eyes roll to the left, as though he's searching for the memory.

'I took an auto rickshaw,' he says, as if it's the most obvious thing in the world.

What idiots we've been, assuming he'd hightailed it away on foot. He's schizophrenic, not stupid.

'Why did you leave?' I say.

He's confused.

'I had to . . . had to . . .' He holds up his hands. I take them. They're covered in dirt, mud embedded under his chipped fingernails.

When I stare at him, his eyes drop to the ground beneath my feet. I follow them. There's a single patch where the mud's even blacker than the surrounding moist, fertile soil.

He's been playing in the dirt.

I lead him back into the house in silence. My salwar is almost soaked through and my braid swings like wet rope against my back. Acha obeys mutely when I order him to wash the dirt from his hands. Voices sound from the drawing room and I follow them to find the family sitting stiffly together, living versions of the stern photos of our relatives on the walls behind them.

'He's here,' I say.

My aunt leaps up. 'Where?' she says. I point back towards the bathroom and she hurries past me to meet him as he emerges. My grandfather sits expressionless.

Acha enters with my aunt as thunder crashes through the night air. He's dry and clean, and has found a burnt-yellow shirt that he wears over his lungi.

'I've told Deepak,' my aunt says. 'He's on his way home now.'

We settle Acha in a chair. I bring fresh water from the kitchen, and the lukewarm, cardamom-flavoured drink that soothes my father but I find disgusting. We sip without speaking, the TV providing ambient noise, until my uncle appears. His face lights up when he sees his brother. He crosses the room, claps him on the back, smiles at his wife.

'I'm glad you called when you did,' he says. 'I was at the police station.'

My grandfather stirs. 'The police station? You told them about this?'

'Yes, Acha,' my uncle says. 'We had to tell them he was missing, especially because he's . . . vulnerable.'

I feel Sanjana looking at me, but I'm staring at my grandfather. His face has hardened.

'So now everybody knows,' he says. For the first time this week, he looks directly at Acha. 'What were you doing, you idiot? You mad fool?'

There's an intake of breath as my grandfather stands and steps towards him, a hand raised. I move in front of him without thinking.

'Acha!' my uncle barks.

We all freeze into awkward, ominous silence. My skin is burning. I feel the blood rushing to my cheeks, hot as lava. My grandfather's eyes move down to mine and his face twists.

'Let's all sit down and have some chai,' my uncle says.

I want to laugh, a raging laugh. He sounds like a souvenir in some tacky shop in Soho, *Keep Calm and Drink Tea*. From the corner of my eye I see my aunt start, turn and disappear into the kitchen.

My grandfather's hand lowers. Light glints in his eye, tracks down to tremble at his lower eyelid. 'I'm going to bed,' he says. He exits with a speed that belies his eighty-five years, shoulders only slightly hunched, head high, unassailable.

The door closes behind him and I turn to Acha. He looks back at me, uncomprehending, like a wounded child.

My aunt returns with the tea. Steam spirals into the humid air above the steel tumblers. She urges us to sit down.

The words pushing impatiently behind the barrier of my teeth are going to cause pain to the wrong people, but I can't hold them back.

'I don't think we should stay here anymore.'

I'm looking at Acha, but I'm speaking to everyone else. When my gaze flicks to them, I see their shame and shock – and relief.

My aunt approaches me, her arms reaching out to wrap around my shoulders. A second later, I'm crying, and Sanjana is there, too, stroking my back. My uncle tries to dissuade me, but I can see his heart isn't in it. He can't change his father. Finally, he calls a hotel he knows, some four-star luxury. He'll drive us there in the morning, he says. And he insists that he'll pay.

'We'll visit you every day,' he says. 'Next time, come to Bangalore. Stay with us.'

He looks at Acha when he speaks. I see the awkwardness and guilt on his face, that he can no longer understand the younger brother he grew up with, that he can't help him.

I feel as though my father's been banned from his ancestral home, from his family's history.

I put him to bed. He looks exhausted following his exertions, but he doesn't sleep, staring at a ceiling that, in the darkness, looks distant as a starless sky. I stand for a while, looking down at him. I can't leave. Sitting down on the floor, my back to the bed, the sharp wooden edge of the frame digging into my spine, I pull out my phone. The world beyond, flickering through the hazy Wi-Fi, pulls me away from my thoughts.

'Maya?' His hand is on my hair.

I turn and wriggle around until I'm on my knees by the bed, as though in prayer. The whites of Acha's eyes gleam at me in the scant moonlight that filters through the window.

'I haven't finished my story, little one.'

I want to tell him to sleep, but I want to hear his voice more.

'The singing maid. The whole household loved her. The other servants. The children, who no longer had their mother to hug. Their father, too. He loved her even more after his wife had drifted off on the smoke of a funeral pyre.

'Then, something changed. She wasn't happy anymore. Her singing no longer echoed from the walls. Now it was her soft sobbing that floated through the trees. The children gave her helpless kisses, but she had stopped smiling. The servants brought her sweets, and she must have eaten them, because her stomach grew rounder every week. The children's father spoke to her too, even getting angry with her. But still she became quieter, shrinking into sadness even as her stomach got bigger, and the father avoided her, as though she had a disease. Then one day, she was gone altogether.'

He's returned to staring at the ceiling and I'm as transfixed by his storytelling as I was as a five-year-old.

'She'd gone to get married, they said. But the younger boy didn't believe she could leave him. He went looking for her that night and he found her. Dressed in her white cotton sari, in the mango tree. Hanging. The rope creaking in the wind.'

He falls silent. I feel sick. 'Acha?' I ask, an odd tightness in my throat. 'What did . . . what did the boy do?'

Acha looks at me. 'He ran back to tell his father,' he says. 'The father told him to go to bed, but he didn't. He followed him in sneaking secret to the mango tree, and watched him dig. Watched her disappear into the ground. He never told anyone, not even his older brother, what he had seen.'

His face crumples. 'He told me it was a dream,' he says. 'Just a dream.'

I place a hand on his cheek, feeling the rough stubble under my palm. He lifts his hand to cover mine. We stay like that until exhaustion drags his lids down and his arm falls limp to the mattress.

I leave him snoring, and I hope he's dreamless. The house is heavy with empty darkness. I walk through it, bare feet soundless. At the door to my bedroom, I stop, and my swirling thoughts fall into a mad decision.

The huge archaic bolt on the front door scrapes free.

The rain's passed. It's pleasantly cool now. As I stray from the path, mud embraces my toes over my sandals, and the grass paints water drops onto my salwar trousers. I step slowly, trying not to think about cobras and cockroaches.

Head down, head down, until the mango tree looms above me. I look up into its branches, feeling an electric thrill of fear. The crow's gone, and there's no sign of a young woman with long black hair. Just leaves, trembling with rainwater, and the graceful, curving outlines of ripe fruit.

Acha's scrabbling at the earth had been less like digging

119

and more of a transfer of the rain-softened dirt from one place to another. I've brought with me a trowel, a small, mud-encrusted thing I found lying by the side of the front porch. It sinks into the ground with ease, as though it wants to search.

The trowel digs and finds dirt, and more dirt. I dig, ignoring the sting of salty moisture in my eyes, until the trowel hits something less easy to loosen and coax to the surface.

I take a breath and let my hands do the searching. I tug and tug until something breaks free and I can lift it to the light of the rising sun.

Stained white cotton drapes over my fingers.

Sharing Time
Gemma Reeves

When Vicky's son had been in hospital for a month, her sister, Beverley, moved in. They hadn't lived together for twenty-seven years. In the evenings, they watched repeats of eighties detective dramas until the early hours. They often ate ice cream for dinner. Beverley put a stop to Vicky sleeping in her son's room and for the last five months they've shared her double bed. At night, Vicky lay awake, listening to Beverley's snores, trying to avoid the twitch of her heavy legs beneath the covers.

This morning, like every morning, she showered, oiled her body, put on clean clothes. She powdered her face, coated each of her pale lashes with black, rubbed a pink balm into her lips. She joined the traffic which stretched along the three-mile route to the hospital. Homerton High Street, Wick Road. She always held her breath as she turned onto Victoria Park Road, but chose not to avoid it. The leaves of the beech trees sagged with rain. Pink and white blossoms were carried away by the wind. She turned on the radio to drown out the windscreen wipers. At Raven Row, she paid for parking. The hospital's blue-glass building was seventeen storeys. Whenever she felt panicky, she sat in her car and counted them – bottom to top, top to bottom.

She didn't need to ask for directions anymore. The corridors all looked the same, but it was a maze she'd cracked. The canteen ladies kept her almond milk in their fridge. She greeted everyone by first name. They replied in kind. Hi Victoria. Hi Victoria. Morning Victoria. All right Victoria – make sure you're getting some rest.

At 9.00 a.m., the whole hospital gleamed. Her son's bed was at the end of the ward next to the window. Vicky stepped into his bay. His long body was motionless beneath the sheets. Each time she saw him, she heard Beverley's voice: *At least they didn't get his face.* 'Hello baby,' Vicky said, stroking his forehead. 'Ready to wake up yet?' She said the same thing every morning, hoping he'd learn through repetition. The almond-shaped eyes he inherited from his father stayed shut, but she could hear him breathing faintly above the sound of the monitors, above the murmured conversations of nurses, patients and visitors.

On the days when his college friends visited, they stood by the bed, unsure where to look, unsure of what to do. They were shocked by the state of his hands and neck, the parts of his chest exposed by his gown. Vicky would ask them to talk, tell stories. She was clingy with the friends she'd already met, worse with the ones who were strangers. She was desperate for clues about his life outside of their home. She knew he was outspoken, hyperactive, a ball of energy. But she discovered he drank much more than she thought he did. That he had two girls in tow, both younger than him. Neither had come to visit. She took this personally, denied the opportunity to yell at them for being selfish. No one could tell her what he was doing in the park that day, so no matter how many times she went back to that morning, she still could not imagine ways to prevent it happening. Guilt was stuck on a loop, like the train track he played with as a toddler.

The details she did know haunted her: he ran from his attacker, and the dazzling pain sent him flying backwards over a bench. Hands protecting face, then clutching torso. The thud of head on kerb. Left arm bent beneath and broken. Out cold. Three or four seconds of blind panic; six months in a coma and counting.

When the police came to her nursery she'd dropped the tray of afternoon snacks. The floor was a mess of yogurt and fruit. The officer said: Acid can be used in robberies, burglaries, revenge attacks, during thefts of mopeds, or to intimidate witnesses. It can be used on spurned lovers, during domestic disputes, in acts of religious or racial hatred. Please think hard, they urged her. Does he have the latest iPhone? Does he attend college? Who are his friends? Is there anyone who might have a vendetta against him? Is he involved in any gangs? Is he known to take or deal drugs? What they were really asking was: How well do you know your son? Implied: Did he have this coming to him? She'd stood there, quiet. Finally she said, 'Who is the suspect here?'

'Morning Victoria,' a nurse said, breezing in with a clipboard. She was a locum and Vicky couldn't remember her name, but appreciated the woman had learnt hers. The nurse checked the tubes, his blood pressure, and emptied his catheter. Vicky didn't look away. She knew her son's body better than she had in a decade.

To his right, separated from him by a thin blue curtain, was Naomi's daughter. She'd been in hospital for even longer than her son. Vicky could hear her waking up, greeting the nurse and asking for water. She'd do anything to hear her son's voice, for his eyes to flip open, for him to sit bolt upright in bed, say, 'All right Mum? Where am I?' In short, she wanted a Hollywood ending. In reality, the longer he was here, the less likely he was to wake and be able to say anything at all. He'd never scored more than a six on the Glasgow Coma Scale. She spent hours waiting for something to happen anyway. Time outside the hospital was too thick, too slow, too full of worry.

Vicky and Naomi had sat side by side for months. They'd seen dozens of people come and go. They'd shared the soundtrack of puking, wailing, emergency alarms activated. It had been quieter in the ICU, but they both agreed that the routine of the ward was preferable. December and January had been the worst months. Shitty weather, moments of touch and go for Naomi's daughter. Vicky liked to think that she and Naomi were united by their strength, but she suspected the glue was their fear.

She'd given up her job at the nursery when the compassionate leave ran out. She packed a box of her things: aluminium water bottle, four Tupperware boxes with three mismatched lids, folders of craft materials. She stole several pots of PVA glue, the kind with a paint stick attached to the lid, and a twelve-by-twelve scrapbook album with forty white pages. She peeled off the 'acid and lignin free' sticker on its cover. She took out a loan.

'Keep up your interests,' Naomi suggested. 'Find new ones.' So Vicky read medical papers on brain trauma, articles on Generation Z masculinity. She joined online forums for coma survival patients. She knew it wasn't what Naomi meant at all. They were useless activities, attempting to unwind time, to ping it back to being linear. Only occasionally would she give up and surf her usual beauty forums, gorge herself on make-up tutorials. She searched for the best deals on city breaks, planned dozens of trips, and then stopped at the page prompting her to enter card details.

She looked up statistics. The UK had one of the highest rates of acid attacks in the world. In London, the worst year for attacks saw 465 recorded. There had been a consistent rise in the number of alt-right sites and blogs that linked acid attacks to Muslims, Asians and migrants. But only six per cent of all suspects in London over the last fifteen years were Asian. First she was surprised by the existence of her own prejudice, and then she was filled with rage. The number 465 buzzed in her head. Her son, only one of hundreds of victims out there. Did they have anything in common?

So she began scrapbooking. It was a routine of sorts. She'd open a bottle of lager, listen to the hiss of gas escape. Sometimes she read the papers; sometimes she searched online and printed her findings. She was careful as she cut. The snip of scissors as they sliced through paper, the faint tang of glue as she stuck the stories onto the white page. She filed away the details, storing them so she could cross-reference each case, storing them so they'd keep out of the folds of her brain where they might linger and burn.

> *An aspiring model and her cousin were sprayed with acid through their car window. On social media, the attack was labelled a hate crime conducted by white supremacists against Muslims. No evidence was found that this was the case. The attacker handed*

> *himself in two weeks later, confessing to*
> *hearing voices in his head.*

The back of the scrapbook was for clippings about her son. Updates about new leads; stories about the lack of updates. There was nothing recent.

Somewhere on the ward an emergency alarm was activated. Outside was grey and wet. In the yellow half-light of the ward she asked him, 'Does it hurt? Are we managing your pain?' There was a time when plasters and Savlon did the trick. She still carried both in her handbag.

At 10.00 a.m., Nina did the checks. She was the most palatable nurse on the ward. Talia was so nice that Vicky couldn't bear talking to her. She preferred Nina because she was decidedly unsympathetic. She had cropped black hair, a blunt fringe, and was direct to the point of impatience. Plus she smoked. She'd once found Vicky weeping in the car park, slumped in her seat, legs half in, half out of her car, and removed her cigarette from her mouth to say, 'Music can help. We had a woman who played her husband's favourite songs every day. It helped connect her to him. Use the playlists from his phone.'

His iPhone had never been recovered, but Nina didn't know that. Vicky found his iPad in the second drawer of his bedside table. She scrolled through his Spotify, locating the most recently played. She discovered he only listened to hip-hop. She couldn't follow the lyrics, couldn't distinguish between artists. So she educated herself. In total, she and Beverley watched fifteen hours of a history of rap series on Netflix. Beverley made proper popcorn in a saucepan on the hob. Each time a kernel hit the glass lid, Vicky winced. They slathered the lot in melted butter and salt flakes and then ate it in place of dinner.

She never knew that Tupac's mother was a Black Panther. She listened to the song *Brenda's Got a Baby* on repeat until she couldn't stop shaking at the lines 'She had it on the bathroom floor . . . She didn't know what to throw away and what to keep'. In an old magazine article she found online, Tupac talked about whether he considered it to be a political song. She read the article twice, trying to feel closer to her son, but the only part she could remember was Tupac's statement that one person's problems can affect a whole community. How it's usually the innocent ones who get hurt.

She checked the iPad's history. It was full of wrestling porn. She watched the videos for an entire hour, thrilled and full of lust, before she deleted the thread. She waited for the shame to kick in but it didn't. Her cheeks flushed with heat. Her body was too responsive.

This morning, she sat through thirty-five minutes of hip-hop as she read the day's papers aloud. She was more informed about the outside world than she'd ever been. The irony of this was not lost on her. The headline: *Former UN climate envoy joins an ever-growing list of experts frustrated by Britain's lack of leadership on carbon emissions*. She twirled the now long tufts of her son's hair around her fingers as she read. He'd like his hair this long. The next page was about the latest boom in Sri Lankan restaurants, where to find a good kottu roti in London. In the background, Monie Love and Queen Latifah were rapping about the power of being a woman. Vicky had grown quite fond of them, but as the song ended she decided to cheat and select her own playlist. 'Sorry baby,' she said, touching her nose to his forehead. Blur, then

Elastica, then Suede blared out. She remembered fucking to Pulp's *Sheffield: Sex City* with his father one night. Red-wine calm, warm skin, the marble wing of his hipbones.

She woke from a nap when Nina began the midday checks. She'd stopped wearing a watch, and followed Nina's timetable of tasks gratefully. Nina froze and turned to look at Vicky. 'His right foot moved away from my hand. Just slightly, an inch, maybe.'

Vicky stood and the iPad clattered to the floor.

'When?'

'Just now.'

'Further than last time?'

'Yes. It could be nothing, but it could be a localised response,' Nina said. 'I'm going to tell the consultant.' She left the ward.

To no one Vicky said, 'Stay calm. Stay calm. Stay calm.'

> *A nurse went to visit her daughter's grave. She sat on a bench to rest and reflect. Nearby, a dispute about drugs was taking place. A bottle fell to the ground and was kicked away. The liquid hit the woman's face, arms, upper body and lower legs. Eleven days later, she died of sepsis relating to her burns.*

All of Vicky's energy was spent holding herself upright, arms folded across chest, fingertips digging into flesh, trying to ignore the smell of ammonia, trying not to lean into a future, because what a betrayal hope had become.

Nina returned. 'It could be hours before the consultant is

free. There's been an accident, a motorway pile-up on the A12. We'll keep monitoring him for any more changes.'

Time passed. She fell into a deep exhaustion, as if trying to reach her son in sleep.

'Knock knock,' Naomi joked before pulling the curtain aside. She was clasping a tin-foil package shaped like the neck of a swan. 'Flapjacks,' she said, with her soft, liquid voice. 'Rocky road topping.' Vicky was surprised to find it was still lunchtime. Naomi worked for a catering company. Her clothes smelled of the outside world: baked bread, fried potatoes, caramelised sugar. She was petite, toned, and always looked attractive – perhaps because her skin was glowy, or maybe because she always brought food.

They'd made a pact that remembrance should not become a catalogue of losses. But in hushed tones they dished the dirt on the fathers. The ones who didn't stick around. Vicky almost loved Naomi because she was tender and friendly and her daughter was on her way out and Vicky's son still might wake up and oh God oh God it felt good not being the one who was worse off for once.

She was too hopeful to tell Naomi about her son's foot. What if she was punished for her excitement and jinxed it? So she swallowed down the news. They sat and talked intermittently on the blue-plastic chairs positioned between the two beds. Naomi's daughter was asleep with music in, white, wireless buds a too-bright extension of her jaundiced ears.

'Weirdest thing he ever put in his mouth as a kid?' Naomi asked. 'Hers was a Sylvanian Families figure. Remember those?'

'When he was nine he was obsessed with licking washing powder,' Vicky replied. 'I found him in the laundry cupboard, clutching a box of Fairy to his chest, licking his fingers. When I asked why, he said, "I wanted to know how clean tastes."'

Stray oats fell from Naomi's lips as she listened. She was wearing textured workout leggings and the flakes gathered in the webbing.

'When he was thirteen, he went vegan for a year. Mealtimes were so tricky I almost hated him,' she confessed to Naomi, who laughed. 'But then I'd remember how when he was five, he told me that he'd grow up and marry me. And I'd forgive him,' she added.

They discussed recipes. 'I'll make jalapeño cornbread tomorrow,' Vicky said. 'We holidayed in Cancún when he was fifteen. He loved the food. Stomach like an ox.' Smell was as important as sound, the consultant had said. Vicky hoped food smells could be the thing that woke him all the way up.

'As a baby, he'd smell like sweet oat milk from the baths I gave him for eczema,' she told Naomi, straying off topic. 'Then one day, he was all Lynx Africa. Eucalyptus from his spot gel.'

This came out as a rush of words, too fast.

When the flapjacks were finished, Naomi kissed her daughter's forehead and left for work. Vicky drew the curtain around her son. She wondered whether to shave his stubbly cheeks. So far, she'd left that to the nurses, afraid of nicking the flesh. She pulled back the sheets, examined his thighs – the source of his multiple grafts, covered now with great swathes of livid skin. Dr Kraicer had told her the prolonged coma did him a favour. With Vicky's consent, they could perform the necessary skin grafts while he was unconscious and skip the painful recovery. 'And,' the junior doctor continued, 'when he wakes up, the skin will already be healing.'

'When?'

'What?'

'When will he wake up?'

He flashed a desperate look at the consultant.

She gave her consent.

She knew they'd used a scalpel, but she'd imagined the surgeon cutting the skin with scissors – like she does with news stories – using neat controlled snips. In her mind, they'd pasted the squares of smooth skin with glue that looked just like PVA. The nurses covered the borrowed areas with Kaltostat, a seaweed-like dressing that helps stop any bleeding, and on top went a piece of padded gauze, wool and bandages. The whole lot stayed there for two weeks. The Kaltostat acted as an artificial scab for him, becoming stiffer with time. This was, apparently, a more painful sensation than the wound itself. He'd never know. She'd imagined it as like being covered in plaster of Paris, feeling it tighten unbearably around her legs as she tried to walk.

She bent to rest her head against the healed patches. 'You are an excellent runner,' she told his legs, feeling her own warm breath return to her. 'My God you are fast. Do you remember sports day last year at college? You were a whir around that huge track. I couldn't get a seat close enough to the front to photograph it.' She took out her phone to watch an old blurry video of that day, as if to confirm that it really happened.

Her son's legs were long and lean like her own. She picked up a bottle of lotion, tipping the white cream into her hands and massaging his legs with antibacterial pharmacy moisturiser. She took extra care with his feet. She had to believe that he could feel her touch the same way she knows he heard her voice reading to him in the womb. His toenails needed clipping. She fetched nail scissors from his toiletry bag. White half-moons fell on the linoleum.

Sleet hit the ward's window. She sighed. She was silently cheering on the explosion of spring. She wanted things in the earth to wake up, to turn green. She trained her gaze on his body, waiting for it to move again. 'Why would you move for Nina, and not for me?' she whispered venomously. 'Please,' she added. 'It's time.' Then she apologised, gently touching the skin on his torso and neck, the places where it had hardened. It felt like cracked soil after months of drought, like bark. Even after all the grafts, there was nothing soft, or lifelike about it. The skin was unrecognisable. It didn't belong to her boy. It had more in common with the park.

> *A two-year-old boy suffered burns to his face*
> *when acid was thrown while he was sitting*
> *in his pushchair in a park. His mother and*
> *father, who had been taking the toddler for*
> *a walk, were also hurt. The boy recovered,*
> *with partial burns to his face. Nobody has*
> *ever been arrested.*

Nina reappeared. 'He's going to be a while,' she said of the consultant. She looked at Vicky's son. 'We've got him on obs every fifteen minutes.'

Vicky stared at her blankly.

'You should give yourself a break. It's not good to be this tense. You know what happened last time. If anything changes we'll call you.'

Vicky ran a finger across her son's eyebrow to smooth the

hairs down. Then she nodded and, although reluctant, kissed her son's cheek, inhaled his sour exhale, and left.

Outside, the weather was like a wet washcloth pressed against her skin. She pulled up her hood and ran to the car. As she drove, she mentally raided the fridge and decided to make carrot and ginger soup. At lunchtime, the journey took ten minutes. She navigated recklessly through the quiet streets. Leaves hit the windscreen. It hadn't stopped raining all month. Her clothes smelled damp even when they were dry.

At home, Beverley was at the kitchen table, typing on her laptop. Vicky resented how she didn't even need to go into her office, how her sister's children were grown-up and at university, living their lives. She called out hello but then saw her scrapbook on the table. She must have forgotten to put it back behind the cookbooks. Beverley looked up at her and said, 'What *is* this?'

'That's mine.'

Beverley shook her head slowly, sadly. 'I don't get it. Are you trying to make yourself feel better? Feel worse?'

Vicky swallowed. 'I'm trying to understand who gets attacked. The different types of people. There'll be patterns between cases, things that link them. It's easier to see when they're all stuck in one place.'

Beverley closed the book. 'It's just . . . a bit sick, Vicky.'

'I'm trying to understand.' Vicky stopped, waiting for a response. 'I need answers,' she continued, louder this time. 'There's so much I don't know.' She heard her voice go up another notch.

She opened the fridge, gathered a handful of carrots, and peeled them methodically over the bin. As she chopped, she recalled all the times in her life that Beverley had pissed her off. When they were small, the silent pinching in dark cinemas with their mum; the way she pretended not to know her at school; how she flirted with Vicky's first boyfriend; how condescending she'd been when Vicky gave birth, how she'd almost gloated over Vicky doing it alone. Not that Beverley's marriage lasted the course. She added the ginger and remembered every single piece of patronising advice Beverley had ever doled out.

And then she remembered that first month when Beverley moved in and had to bathe her. Beverley had always been much bigger, with strong, wide thighs, but she managed to sit on the edge of the tub, and she sang the same songs their mother used to sing, and the water slid off Vicky's back, warm and cleansing.

'Lunch is ready,' she called out, her voice strained.

They ate in silence until Beverley said, 'You're losing your figure. You're all skin and bones.' She got up, found the iPad, and downloaded a fitness app, paying for the Home Transformation Guide. They watched the intro video. Vicky stared at the young trainer's skin, tanned and smooth and blemish-free; her abs were so defined they looked drawn on. She felt good at the prospect of exercising again: she could be energetic, quick, nimble – like her son. Like her son had been. They cleared a space in the living room, and Vicky rolled out her yoga mat. They collapsed into a fit of giggles trying to do burpees.

Sweating on the floor and staring up at the ceiling, she told Beverley that he moved his foot this morning. There was a pause and then Beverley thanked God in a suppressed but urgent manner that Vicky found very worrying. She'd never heard her sister address any kind of God before. It took away from the moment, and she was frightened again, of false alarms, of hope dried up.

Afterwards, Vicky settled into an armchair, put on her son's headphones and tuned into her favourite true-crime podcast. She rested her phone on the arm of the chair in case the hospital called, and then relaxed as the presenter's voice rushed into her ears with other people's problems. The sound quality was so good that she once Googled the brand of headphones and discovered they cost two hundred pounds. She had no idea where her son found that kind of money. She decided to leave that thought there.

There was no phone call from the hospital.

> *The boyfriend of a reality TV star threw*
> *acid across an east London club, wounding*
> *twenty people. His defence was that he*
> *thought the bottle contained a liquid date-*
> *rape drug which he had snatched from two*
> *men after overhearing them plan to spike*
> *a girl's drink. He was sentenced to twenty*
> *years in prison.*

Early evening, she drove back to demand news from the consultant. Beverley wanted to join her, but when her son's left eye had flickered Beverley came with her and then nothing changed. So Vicky said she'd go alone, thank you very much. She was stuck in traffic for a long time and when she moved through the last set of lights, dusk had happened.

The hospital looked larger at night, more geometric. A different beast. Talia was on duty. Her hair was swept up onto the top of her head and teased into the shape of a bow. She told Vicky the consultant was still busy with the car-collision victims. 'He hasn't made it onto the ward yet,' she said, 'but he'll come as soon as he can.' Vicky glared at Talia. She could wring her neck. She could almost hear it crack. She blamed Talia personally for the hold-up. 'I'll wait for him,' she told her defiantly, though what she was defying really, she didn't know. Talia gave her a half-smile. 'It could be a couple of hours,' she said.

Naomi returned to the ward after her catering job finished. She gave Vicky a hot chocolate from the vending machine at the other end of the hall. They blew across their cups and sipped, taking turns to divulge the irritating things their children did. There was the usual litany of gripes: wet towels left on the floor, cotton rounds flushed not thrown and the drainpipes clogged. Vicky said, 'I've never seen anyone take more pleasure in burping. He loves to let it rip. You know when they're newborns and pass gas with their whole body? He's still like that – it rolls up through his stomach and out of his mouth.'

Naomi laughed.

'And when he was fifteen, he started thanking me for telling him off. I'd hold up the mud-stained running kit he'd just dumped on the floor, and say something like, "You know, I wasn't born just to pick up after your mess," and he'd reply, "Thank you for telling me, Mum," with this unbearable smirk on his face.'

When Naomi fell asleep, Vicky went to the nurses' station. They were laughing. Before she could open her mouth, Talia put down her lip balm, tucked a flyaway hair behind her ear and told Vicky that the consultant would be there as soon as he could. 'Go stretch your legs,' Talia said. 'Get some air.'

Vicky nodded; she'd go for a walk, but she had no intention of leaving the building. It was easy to wander anywhere in the hospital at night. All corridors were fair game. She slipped through doors in the sticky delay before they properly closed. She liked the grey, functional store cupboards, the way they were divided by ailments. The occupational therapy and physiotherapy rooms were always empty and smelled like hand sanitiser. She took a seat in the relatives' lounge, stared at the magnolia walls. A pink silk orchid bothered her to distraction – if a real orchid couldn't survive in hospital then what could?

She headed downstairs to A&E to spy on the traumas. A balding man with a bleeding head was drinking from a paper bag. An elderly woman in a thin yellow dress was crying, her husband whispering into her ear. Four teenagers, eyes trained on one phone, silently watched something unfold, mouths agape. They were all lucky to have minor injuries – to not be crumbling day by day, week by week, personality hidden away, morphing and shifting beneath the eyelids. She didn't stay there long. The memory of the day of the attack rose to the surface, and she could see her own body in the rows of people waiting. But that couldn't be right: they hadn't had to wait.

When she returned to the ward, Naomi was crying. It didn't happen often anymore but when the gates opened it was a flood. Vicky comforted her, feeling smug and capable until her own eyes began to brim.

Naomi left. There was still no sign of the consultant. Vicky itched with impatience. Talia was too busy to stop and talk, so she settled in the chair by her son's bed, all her nerves fired up, alert, watching for movement. Behind his body was the window: the smack of rain, and ambulance lights flashing blue and then disappearing. She listened to the hum of machines and could almost hear the tick of minutes as they passed; each one lost to him. Another, then another, then one more.

The Bread Man
Kevin Dyer

He is clearly foreign. Clearly not from round here.

His clothes are not the best. He is a traveller. Unshaven.
But his hands are immaculately clean. Odd that.

'Hello,' he says.

Normally you can find out a lot from a 'Hello': where they
are from, what they want, are they rich, are they begging, are
they scared.

But this was a 'Hello' the people in the disused garage had not
heard before. It sort of said: 'Don't mind me I'm going to do
something but it's not going to hurt you and then I'll be gone.'

Then he says, 'The roads were . . .' but he doesn't finish the
sentence, just shrugs, because everyone knows what the roads
are like. Shit and broken. Full of holes and not going to be
fixed until it's all over.

The people watch him. They can see he hasn't got a gun or a
bomb. He carries stuff in from outside and places it on a large

tarpaulin in the middle of the concrete floor.

A baby in the corner is crying. A woman who isn't its mother makes soothing noises and puts an old punctured dummy in its mouth. The baby is hungry; the woman, not being its mother, has no milk for it.

The man looks at the woman. His eyes say, 'Babies, they cry don't they, it's all right.' And she believes him, somehow, for that instant, even though everyone within a hundred miles knows that it's not all right.

He has brought in a few bags and a big plastic container. Some people think he is going to try and sell stuff.

People bring different things when they arrive.
Some bring suitcases,
some bring bullets and guns.
Some bring long words or plans to change things.
Some bring hate.

He has this:

flour

salt

oil

a little sugar

something in his inside pocket.

And a joke.

'I always carry a joke,' he says, and he gets a little scrap of paper from his pocket. But he can't find his glasses.

'Can I borrow someone's reading glasses? I wrote this joke on this paper a long time ago so I wouldn't forget it and, well, the light was better then.'

Eventually a woman takes a pair from her apron pocket and hands them to him. It isn't because she is being kind now, to this foreign stranger, just that she has always been that way and the habit has not yet been broken.
He smiles. The first in this place for days.

An old, miserable man in filthy clothes and a pair of scrappy leather slippers clears his throat, a scraping of phlegm that sort of says, 'What right has he got to come in here with his smiling.' The clearly foreign man looks at the old, miserable man and nods his head, lowering his eyes. This unspoken male code says, 'I am not a threat, I'll be gone soon, give me a chance, eh?'

The old, miserable man says nothing – which the stranger eventually takes as permission to continue.

He puts on the woman's glasses. He can barely see out of them because the prescription is too strong. In fact, any prescription would be too strong; his eyesight is perfect, he does not wear glasses. Also, he does not need them because he knows the joke by heart; he has said it a thousand times. He's only borrowed the glasses so that after pretending to use

them he can give them back and she and everyone else will know he is not here to take
but to give.

'This might not be the best joke,' he says. 'But at least it's a joke. At times like this, we need a joke, don't we?'

No one says yes.

A child farts. No one cares.

The old man clears his throat again. It means, 'Piss off with your jokes.'

Yesterday the hospital was targeted and everybody knows the planes did it on purpose. It is the seventh hospital in the city blasted and burned in seven days. All the bakeries have already been hit.

The city is a killing ground. The last haven, they thought; the place where they'd let everyone who disagreed, everyone who had been the mother or a brother or a child of a rebel sit it out until the soldiers went and the politicians came and sorted it out. This is the place they brought everyone to from the other places they had bombed to nothing. They came here on the green buses that the government paid for, escorted by soldiers with guns but watched by the Red Crescent and men and women in nice clothes from the UN. All the kids were given a bag of sweets, all the adults two litres of best foreign water. It was a new beginning, there would be tents and sewers and jobs, but they know now it was and is a trap. The politicians are locked out again and won't be let in until the last bullet has been shot, the last bomb dropped, the last canister of gas thrown in the last doorway.

There are about thirty people in the room, an old garage that used to repair high-end cars. Where the stranger stands used to be a pit where a mechanic in bright-blue overalls worked. He had a silver socket set given to him by his dad when he started his apprenticeship. When the planes came he joined the rebels. He's dead now. The pit is boarded over.

The stranger knows none of this.

He brings out a large battered mixing bowl and wipes the inside with a preciously clean white cloth.

He goes back to the scrap of paper. He tells the joke. A few children nearly laugh. But only because it has the word 'bottom' in it.

He was right; it is not a very good joke, more like one a dad would tell a small child. In fact it is quite a bad joke.

The old, miserable man's face is like a stone. Not because the joke is bad but because this same joke he had told to his own son, before he was a mechanic, before he bought him the blue overalls, before he gave him the silver socket set, before he went away and never came back.

The stranger gets another scrap of paper out of his pocket. A second joke is written on it. He has no intention of saying it; he simply gives the scrap of paper to a man sitting over by a pile of worn tyres. This man, like the rest, has been hiding in the disused garage for the last ten hours waiting for the all-clear. This man is in charge of emptying the piss bucket that steams in the corner behind a curtain. Whether he put himself in charge of this job or someone else put him there is unclear.

At the moment of offering the paper to the man he sees the can-carrier has only one hand. The stranger's mind invents a dozen reasons for the man's disability, but he doesn't allow himself to ask how or why or when.

'Tell it to yourself later when you get home,' he says.

The man accepts it, because in that sentence 'Tell it to yourself later when you get home' is a sort of promise that he will actually get home.

Then he gives the woman her glasses back.

The clearly foreign man is ready. He taps his finger on the top of each container.

'Flour,
oil,
a little salt,
water,
and some sugar.'

Then he pours a little sugar into a small bowl. The children in the room are eager now; they haven't seen sugar for a long time. He licks his finger, puts it in the bowl, then sucks the sugar off his finger – not because he wants it but as an example to the kids, showing them what the rules are.

He passes the bowl to one of the older girls, trusting her to do it as prescribed.

'Just lick, one dip, then pass it on.'

The girl puts her finger far into her mouth, wetting as much of it as she can. Then she dips it in the bowl as deep as it can go, getting as many granules to stick as is possible. She carefully lifts her finger out, not dropping a single grain. Stuffs it in her mouth.

Bliss.

'Pass it on,' he says.

She does.

The old garage fills with a buzz of expectation. The stranger tells a boy, 'Just one dip, then pass it on.'

In this place they don't make bread on tables. They do it on the floor in a bowl. The women used to do it like this long before the demonstrations and the reprisals and the invaders from the east and the interferers from the west and the hell that is this country now. On the floor: it's just how they do it.

He puts the bowl on the floor and gets ready to measure the flour, using an old mug with a picture of the Eiffel Tower on it. He has never been to the Eiffel Tower. Nobody in the room has. But everyone knows someone who has passed through France and moved on, or gone to France and been sent back, or gone to France and never been heard of again.

He goes over to the wall and turns the tap.

'Not today,' says the woman who lent him the glasses. 'Not for three days.'

Nothing comes out, not even a gurgle, not even a hiss.

At first, two years ago, when he started doing this, he assumed people would have water, it's a human right after all, but soon found out that in this place nothing can be assumed. Not anymore. So once, just on the edge of Homs, in a suburb called Al-Bayadah, he paid a man 100,000 for an old, battered truck. He didn't want the truck but he needed the two big water tanks in the back, and the truck was the necessary thing to shift them. The tanks had 'UNHCR' stamped on them, but that was no passport to anywhere, no guarantee of anything.

After buying the truck he drove to nowhere and filled up the big tanks at an old well, one bucket at a time. The village was just a pile of bricks way out west in a place that once grew pomegranates and maize but is now just shrapnel scattered between broken things. No one helped him, no one bothered him, no one shot at him, the mad man spending six hours bucketing water from a well in no man's land. Then he drove for three more hours.

In the place he got to, a hall in a village, the children drank, gulping it down. Except one girl; she took a plastic cup of the warm wet water, carried it to the corner and sipped it. He watched her but she didn't see him watching; she was in her own little bubble. Her and the water in the plastic cup . . . sip sip sip. Where she had gone to in her head he didn't know

– maybe to when her papa was still here, maybe to before they took her Aunty Sophie away, maybe to a place in the future with clean sheets and a dog to drag around on a piece of string.

It was time to start; the little sugar bowl was empty.

This is a garage. Was. There is no oven. In fact there's no electricity now. He touched again the flour, salt, oil, water, sugar.

'Can anyone make a fire?'

The answer came in the silence. No one is going to go outside until the all-clear – except the man who empties the piss bucket and he'll do that silently and only half a pace from the back door. Lighting a fire out there would be like poking a stick into a wasps' nest. Also, they might look like starved, hopeless, shitty, sticks of people, but these are the survivors, the ones who get through. They are not the ones to go outside and get shot because they do something careless, something stupid.

The sugar in the bowl was a stunt they would go along with.
The joke was a stunt they'd go along with.
Lending him a pair of spectacles was a stunt they'd go along with.
But no one will go outside, not until one of the White Helmets comes and tells them it's safe.

'I've got some matches.' So says the young boy who was third in the dipping-finger-in-the-sugar queue.

Of course, the stranger doesn't really want a volunteer to go outside the building. He is just looking for some sort of consent to the event that he is making happen. The boy, unknowingly, by offering a box of matches, has committed the whole group, two and a half dozen frightened, hiding people. The man gives the boy a smile, takes the matches, promises to return them – all bar one – and then picks up an old wooden chair that is lying in the corner.

It is broken now; the seat was pushed through when someone stood on it to hang the curtain round the piss bucket. He breaks it into kindling with his hands. Not by placing it on a step and jumping on it, not by cracking it over his thigh – he just splinters it with his bare hands.

The boy is impressed and lets out a 'Woooh!' His mother clips him round the ear and tells him to be quiet.

'Baker's hands,' the man says, lightening the mood. But in this country where physical might makes the difference between life and death, there is a slight feeling of, just for now, with this man here, being a little less in peril.

He takes the wood outside. There is a frisson in the room. Ten minutes ago this man was an invader; now they are worried for his safety. They are all aware of this shift in themselves and it makes them feel uncertain.

Outside in the dusty back alley the man finds some other scraps of kindling – an old, disused crate, some paper, a handful of dead mimosa leaves. Then there, behind the garage, where the mechanic and his mates used to kick a ball about and pretend to be Messi or Ronaldo or Gareth Bale, he makes a little pyramid of sticks.

He calls back in to the others: 'I like ovens. In fact I could talk about ovens for a long time. I am a sort of oven nerd, you know. Gas, electric, fan-assisted, wood-fired, charcoal, open, metal, brick. There is something romantic about a brick oven, don't you think? I was once in Shir-al-Hain, a tiny place in Iran, and they had a brick oven shaped like an old beehive. The baker man there had dough that was perfect, elastic like a pizza but thin as your shirt, and the oven was hot as hot and I watched him put his hand in, with the dough, and spin the circle of dough up onto the oven roof. It stuck there, up, inside the hot oven, on the roof. Incredible, against all the rules of physics. Anyway, minutes later, just a few minutes, it falls down, perfectly cooked.'

He leaves a pause while he strikes the match and the dead leaves catch.

'My cousin lives in Dagenham, that's in England. It's just like here but with more betting shops. He has a halogen hob.'

The fire is sparking now, the pyramid starting to collapse in on itself, and the old chair, ingrained with oil from the hands of the young mechanic who used to sit on it and drink tea and talk about his hopes and dreams, begins to burn.

The man comes back in. They're all watching him. It is a long time since they saw a man that wasn't running or hiding, bossing or being bossed, killing or being killed.

'Excuse me, will you help me?' he asks one of the women.

'I'm not going outside,' she says flatly.

'And I don't blame you. That wind off the sea is sharp as a knife.'

When he smiles at her, a bit of her, inside, a bit she thought was dead, weeps. In places like this, and times like this, humanity aches for a bit of humanity.

'Will you do this?' He gestures to the bowl. He doesn't wait for a reply. 'I'll do the measuring, you do the next bit, eh?'

He wipes down the mixing bowl again.

'What's your name?' says the woman as she kneels behind the bowl.

'I don't have any scales, I'm afraid. I guess the amounts.'

He never tells his name. Because if, after he has gone, they are asked by someone, it is better they don't know. Better they say: 'We asked him but he didn't tell us.' Better they do not lie trying to keep his name secret. Because liars get found out, liars get beaten, liars get dragged into the alley and shot. If someone comes later they can just say, 'This foreigner' – because he was clearly a foreigner – 'rolled up in some crappy truck. And now he's gone, good riddance.'

And if they get asked about the truck, they can say, 'I don't know, he told us about it but parked round the corner.'

'What about the registration plate?'

'We never saw it, we were in here, shitting our pants.'

In fact there are no registration plates, or if there are, they are smeared with dirt and grime and impossible to read.

Just an old truck, flour, oil, salt, sugar, water
and the baker man.

The people ask: 'What do you want? Where are you from?'

He dips a mug with the Eiffel Tower on it into the large paper sack, and measures out fifteen scoops of flour.

'You kids count with me, I have a terrible memory.'

They do, a sort of game.

'And now some salt.'

He puts in a few generous pinches.

'I collected this from the beaches near the Jordan border, it lies there at high tide on the flat rocks in crisp, white sheets. You just scrape it up with a spoon and take it away. Like people have for a thousand years – like people will still be doing in another thousand years.'

They do not know whether to believe him or not, that you can scrape up salt from the ground with a spoon. They want to, but . . .

'Oil next. This much . . .'

He glugs some in.

'I hope you are remembering, because one day you'll be doing this yourselves.'

He gives the woman a wooden spoon. Actually more of a stick with a slight hollow at one end. Was a spoon, but now worn away by a million mixings.

He pours a little sugar into the bowl.

To the woman: 'You ready?'

'I'm ready.'

And he pulls out from his pocket a paper envelope with dried yeast inside.

'Now the magic stuff.'

He pours the right amount – he knows it exactly – into the bowl that the woman is now mixing in. He didn't need to keep the yeast till last or produce it from his pocket in this way, but he has a sprinkling of showman in him.

He watches her. Her fingers are long and thin. Delicate. Precise. Inside the weathered and worn skin of this woman, surviving and showing all the scars of it, is a beautiful, gentle human being. And when she looks up at him he sees that even more, and she knows he sees it and so feels it herself, for the first time in a long, long time. He isn't flirting with the woman who is working the dough, but he places his hand on her shoulder, against all the rules of behaviour in this part of the world. He does it to say, 'You are a good woman and you do not deserve all this. You are a good woman and I will never forget you for helping me. Never.'

He pours in seven Eiffels of water.

The dry and the wet materials fight with each other, neither one wanting to be the other. But her fingers push them together against their will, until they become an agglomeration, a mass of different shapes and textures to begin with, but eventually one thing.

He drags out an old wok from his bag.

'Back soon.'

The fire is burning well.
He throws on some larger pieces of wood that lie under the bent frame of a cannibalised moped.
He finds some stones and bricks and builds three roughly made legs around the fire, then balances the wok upside down on the three supports, so that it is like a domed roof above the flames.

Inside the woman is still working the dough and the people are talking now – about the man, about the fire, about other things that have long been on their minds but not got as far as their lips.

Outside a man with a gun walks past, looking at the stranger. He shouts at the man kneeling by the wok:

'You! What the fuck?'

Calmly: 'I'm making saj. Want some?'

'Fuck you,' says the man with the gun, and walks off. He cocks the gun. He has his jaw stuck out and his arms look like they are carrying invisible rolls of carpet under them.

It hasn't rained for over two months so the wood is burning fiercely. The upturned wok is too hot to touch.

'We are ready, azizam,' says a voice calling from inside.

He looks up and eyes stare at him from the windows. No glass of course, just holes. The woman stands there, smiling at him. The old, miserable man is just behind her – he has watched and his brain is alive with it all.

The wall has bullet holes, a long line of them running from the bottom corner up across the window and up to the top corner opposite where the printed sign reads 'Idlib Garage' and scrawled in paint 'CLOSED'.

Inside now three women are breaking bits off the main lump of dough and rolling the elasticy dough pieces into balls then slapping them, moving them from hand to hand from small rounds
to small ovals
to saucers

to small plates
to large stretchy dinner-plate-sized discs.

It's like how Italian women make pizza bases or Mexican women make tortillas. A long time ago the baker man thought, 'All over the world we know how to do this. We come together in this. Isn't this thing, that we all make the same bread in the same way, a thing of hope?'

'I couldn't do that,' he says. 'I can't get it to be that thin. It breaks into bits and shoots over the floor.'

The women laugh. 'Men are so useless,' is the unsaid conversation that runs between them.

The three women feel good, being the experts, being praised for what they have done since they were kids when their mothers taught them.

'The fire is good,' says the old man, looking out the window.

People look at him. This is the first time he has spoken in months. Not since the garage closed.

The stranger takes the first three flat circles of dough and goes outside.

He knows he's being watched. But he doesn't look up, just keeps his eyes on the job.

He flops the first one down on the upturned wok.

He takes out an old bone-handled fork which he keeps in his other inside pocket. After a minute he checks the underside by lifting the edges resting on the wok, now an improvised convex cooking slab. He does this without burning his fingers and with the skill of a man who has done this many times before.

He lied to the women. He can make bread anyhow anywhere with anyone. In village halls, in burnt-out mosques, in caves in the hills, under plastic sheets at the edge of a forest, anywhere. This is what he does. This is his calling.

He flicks it over, barely a minute gone, and the one side is done. The mottling on it looks like the craters of the moon. It has a beautiful, unique pattern that only this piece of bread has – different to the million, million other flatbreads ever made in the world since the beginning of time.
And now the second side is done.

The soldier with the jaw and the invisible carpets and the gun comes back. He stands there, full square, knowing full well he is the power and this is his place.

'Yours will be ready in a few minutes,' says the baker man. 'Actually the people are too scared to come out, would you help me take it inside?'

The man with the gun is in no way going to go inside the garage. He is the toughest in the street, but fear is as thick in his blood as anyone else's. He spits in the dust, wipes his lips with the back of his hand. On his neck is tattooed the word 'Kristina'.

Everyone now can smell the burning wood and the baking saj.

The old man comes out of the garage.

'I'll be the waiter.' And he laughs at his own joke – that there could be a waiter in this dead place with no cafés, no restaurants, no food.

'When I was a child I wanted to be a waiter in Damascus,' he says, 'but my father made me stay home. He said there was a good life to be had here.' He snorts at the absurdity of such an idea. He takes the first saj, a perfect circle of perfect bread as thin as the finest French crêpe.

So they make a little assembly line: the foreigner baking at the improvised oven, three women handling the dough, the old man who hadn't spoken bringing out the uncooked rounds and taking back the cooked ones. He passes them to the woman with the reading glasses who distributes them.

'Children first,' says the old man to the baker – but really saying it to the man with the gun who is dragging on a cigarette just to show how hard he is.

But the boy looking through the crack in the door knows that isn't true. He knows that it is the man with the oil and the flour and the yeast that is in control here. Not for long maybe, but for now, yes, for now.

The women carry on kneading and spinning the circles of saj. When the old, not miserable anymore man offers them

cooked bread they say, 'Not for me, give it to the others first.'
This, even though they have eaten nothing for three days.

The fire burns, the children eat, the women talk.

Then, eventually: 'This one's yours,' says the baker to the
man with the gun.

In another place in another time someone would have said to
the man with the AK-47, 'Nice gun.' But not here, not now.

He hands him some bread.
He doesn't expect a thank you.
He doesn't get one.
The man with the gun smells the bread. He lives a stale life
where he is suspicious of everything and everyone. That isn't
going to change because some hot, fresh, perfect bread gets
passed his way.

But . . .

'It's good,' says the man with the gun whose girlfriend is two
thousand kilometres away.

'Want another?'

The man nods. He is hungry and the taste makes him think
of Kristina in a town a day north of St Petersburg. He doesn't
cry, of course he doesn't, but he lets out a sigh that the little
boy hears and the woman hears and the baker hears.

And the stranger gives him a second beautiful moon-patterned circle of piping-hot saj bread. Yes, they smell a bit of woodsmoke, yes they'd be better with Nutella or hummus or rolled with goats' cheese or served on a plate in a café by the beach. But not much.

'That's the lot,' says the first woman who helped.

The old man brings out the last three uncooked pieces.

The last three circles of dough are laid one at a time onto the wok.

The women watch them cook one by one, standing in the doorway like girls.

They all watch them brown and mottle.

The baker man lifts the edges and flips them over.

The man with the gun says:

'Fucking good bread, baker man.' And the women laugh, knowing it is true even before the warmth of it touches their lips.

The old man passes over the last three moons to the three women. He calls them madam and apologises for his dirty hands.

They eat, determined not to look at the urine and turds in the wheel ruts by the back door.

The woman inside has chewed some of the bread to a mush and is putting it in the baby's mouth with her fingers.

Then. All gone. The stranger kicks the wok off the fire and, while it cools, packs the rest of his gear back into the truck. And the wind blows, and dust comes in off the street into the garage.

When he comes back, the man with the gun hands him the wok. It is still hot and is burning his fingers, so he passes it from one hand to the other distributing the heat.

The baker with his baker's hands takes it as if it was not hot at all, just normal. Normal. Because that's what all this is – the bullet holes, the people crouching in a disused piss-smelling garage, the streets empty except for men with guns.

The girl finds a single grain of sugar still caught under her fingernail.

The old man thinks of his son.

A little boy pees in the bucket behind the curtain.

Spiders

Andrea Watts

The spiders arrived while I was sleeping. Spun fine threads that criss-crossed wall to wall. The next night there were more, and more again each night after that, until they covered the window in a blur of overlapping universes that hung above my mattress. I watch my breath bounce off them, leaving pinhead dewy gems. My bed is under the eaves on the mezzanine, so close to the sloping ceiling that lying down I can touch it with my toes. Only at the edge can I sit tall. A wooden stepladder with nine treads leads to the kitchenette below: small fridge, oven, two burners and attached to the wall a table that can be collapsed when not in use. As clever as a ship's cabin and damp as an old church, the space is on loan to me while my friend is visiting family in Colombia. She will be gone all winter. Her shed is hard to heat.

I don't know what the spiders want. They are hunched and angry when I raise a hand or foot near them. This makes me sad. Don't they know I would never harm them? It is too cold to put them outside with their collection of corpses. At home we leave chestnuts on windowsills. Spiders don't like the smell and find somewhere else to live. I think it is too late in the year now for chestnuts.

I have been in this country for eighteen months and am already dreaming in English; it has infiltrated my world. I speak to my daughter Alina every evening on the phone. We speak in English. That way she will be prepared when she joins me here. We dance together. She is a very good dancer. Oh-oh-oh she loves Katy Perry and does a terrifying roar. Soon, as soon as I have the right to stay and have saved enough for a place of our own, I will bring her over and she will go to school, learn English, go to university.

I have cleaning jobs as well as making sandwiches for the supermarkets, Tesco, Aldi, Sainsbury's. I didn't like it at first, setting out at 5 a.m., but the people are nice, and the sandwiches are 40 pence, though they do not fill us up. Cleaning pays better and most of my employers are not at home. They give me their keys and their trust, and I can complete the tasks in half the time I am paid for.

Only Phoebe is there when I come, and she is so pleased to see me, she makes me cups of tea. Last Christmas they went to Peru and brought me back a soft and warm woollen cardigan in dark sunset colours. It is too big for me, I have lost weight since I moved here, but when I put it on it is like being wrapped and rocked and swaddled. There are no buttons, just one long zip to keep out the cold. I wear it so much it has bobbled. One day, Phoebe came up behind me and cut off a loose thread. She is very tall and beautiful and carries a penknife in the pocket of her overalls because she is a stone-carver. She has a studio in her garden the size of my shed. I do not clean in there. But once, she showed me inside, showed me the white stone she had carved as a monument for a famous actress I had not heard of. The words so delicately chiselled they made the stone seem vulnerable and pliant. The cardigan is not as practical as a fleece. Phoebe showed me photos of the huts her children and she slept in on a silver beach, and we laughed together to think they had left their big house to sleep in huts.

Before this shed, I shared a canal boat with Byron. The first night I met him, he was so drunk he fell off his stool. He bought me drinks and told me he loved me when I helped him home. His boat was spacious, with two small bedrooms, a tiny bathroom and, in the living area, a wood-burning stove. On the walls, he had hung watercolours of places he had previously lived, which he had painted himself. Twenty years my senior, he made very few demands and showed me corners of England I would never have found. In the summer we camped in wild, remote sites, swam in a river – until we spotted leeches floating in the shallows. I did not join him swimming in the sea. I am afraid of the sea, but I told him simply that it was because it was too cold. That at home the sea is warm. It is a sensible fear, I think. Alina and my mother live in a small seaside town far from where I grew up. Alina isn't scared of the sea. She isn't scared of anything. She hasn't learnt fear, and this is frightening to me. My mother has mellowed with age and indulges Alina. I am afraid my mother won't be paying close enough attention. Alina is the best at math in her class, like my sister who teaches at the high school. I want her here so much. Things are different back home now. No crops are being grown. Foreign companies have built factories for the cheap labour and tax incentives, but the money they pay is not enough for us to live on.

I moved out of Byron's boat to make space for his daughter when she came back from university. It was Byron who introduced me to my friend with the shed. I prefer it on my own and I don't mind the cold so much anymore. He gave me three blankets when I moved in and Phoebe gave me a winter-flowering clematis in a large pot from her garden. She said that the pollen irritated her eyes. I have it by my front door, in a small courtyard hidden from the main road by the surrounding buildings. It is not a bad space and I have got used to the rattling extractor fan from the kebab shop that smells of chips and burnt fat and makes me hungry from midday until late at night. The clematis is doing OK. Perhaps I will plant bulbs for the spring.

I find myself more and more at Phoebe's. She has increased my money from £11 an hour to £13.50, five times the rate I can get at home. And now she wants me every day between three and six, so there will always be someone there when Saskia and Bridie get in from school. They are twelve and fourteen, too old for a babysitter but their father will pay, a famous photographer who recently moved with his new wife to Dublin, where the tax is low. There hasn't been a day that Phoebe is not home to greet the girls with smiles and cookies and questions. They wriggle away, pretending not to care, then kerlumph heavy-footed upstairs leaving a trail of shoes, socks, bags, blazers for me to tidy away. Phoebe's smile is nervous and open and too easily given.

Last Tuesday, when I came downstairs, she was standing on the kitchen table reaching for something on the top shelf. She was wearing only a black bra and cream lace knickers that did not hide anything. There was a large neat scar across her stomach in the shape of a crooked smile, vivid but healing well. I looked away quickly so as not to embarrass her.

And then, somehow, she slipped.

It happened in slow motion, a roll of shiny silver paper

unravelling around her. I was not fast enough to break her fall, and the knock as her head hit the kitchen counter was loud. She landed on her back, legs crumpled under her. There was a terrible silence and then she swore – 'Jesus, fuck' – and touched the back of her head, almost smiled.

'Are you all right?' I said and crouched beside her.

'I'm all right. Give me a minute.'

'Where does it hurt?' I reached out and my bare arm brushed her stomach.

'No!' she shouted and gave me a little shove and kick. 'I'm fine.'

'You're in shock. Please don't move.'

'I'm fine,' she said again. 'I'll be fine. I just need to stay here for a bit.'

'How can I help? What can I do?'

She pointed to the unravelled paper. 'Wrap Saskia's birthday present,' she said.

The next afternoon, she messaged to ask if I minded skipping that day. She had a meeting with a new client and wanted to use the kitchen. I was already on the bus, and instead of going home, I got off and ducked under the railway bridge to the canal. It was cold but bright, the air so sharp it was difficult to breathe. I counted two ducks and two drakes hidden behind overhanging branches on the opposite bank. Lime-green water plants had gathered thickly enough to form an island they could walk on. I wondered if it was safe for them to build a nest.

The days are getting longer. Soon it will be spring, and my friend will return, and I will need somewhere new to live. It was summer when I left home. Alina and I went to the mountains for a few days where it was cooler. We found a glacial pool which Alina jumped into over and over as if she couldn't feel the icy cold. And afterwards, climbing over boulders, she discovered a nursery of long-legged spiders hiding under a rock. So many, a city, a trembling mass, and if you put your hand close to them, they would shiver collectively and bounce up and down. They had no webs and Alina wanted to know what they ate and who was looking after them. Perhaps they would starve.

'Perhaps they don't need food until they are fully grown,' I said. 'Or perhaps they eat at night out of the sun.'

'But where is their mother?' she said. She lay on the rock, belly down, her face so close to the little spiders that after a while they forgot she was there. When it was time to go, I had to gently comb them out of her hair.

Today – Friday – Phoebe isn't here when I arrive to clean. It is a grey day and I can see the light on in her studio, her silhouette at the window. She doesn't come out even when the girls come home. After I leave, she sends a message. Have I moved her credit card? She thought she left it on the kitchen counter, but now can't find it.

No, I reply.

Not to worry, she says.

But then I am not sure. I am tired today, off balance. The walk to the bus stop is louder than usual, the lights more glaring, the pollution worse. Dusty metal dries my tongue, my lips. I hold my breath to hush the nausea. It is busy. I am rushed along by other people. When I first arrived in London, I would sit in St Pancras station where the trains come in from Europe, and watch the new people arrive. This is where I go now. Allow myself to be guided onto the escalator. It is comforting being carried up, hand on rail, prevented from falling by people in front and people behind. It is quiet up here in the eaves of the building. Distant humming engines muffle footsteps and wheelie suitcases. No one speaks as they pass. It is as hushed as a church. Someone has found the piano on the concourse below. Tinkling runs and dead notes.

I sit back against a glass wall opposite a bronze statue of a big-bellied man. He is holding on to his hat, coat flying behind him, as wobbly on his feet as a pigeon. Larger than life. He has so much life. A few tourists gather to have their picture taken by his side, whispering as if they are trespassing. A poet honoured here as if he were a leader, his words carved in a plaque around his feet: *misty sea-line*, *wash of air*. When I was Alina's age, there were only happy things on the radio. Even after Chernobyl, happy things. We looked after the refugees. Food was plentiful. A whole street was built in our town, houses and fields given over to them. Houses, not sheds.

The piano becomes louder. A singer joins in, dark and operatic, but then her song is cut short suddenly; or is too quiet to hear above the engines. I shut my eyes. An arc of white light and coloured zigzags float behind them. Once, Byron took me to a large gallery made of iron and glass. Inside, a giant spider hovered on needle-tipped legs. I crouched under her in a silent scream so he could take my photo like I'd just dropped from her sac of eggs. I sent it to Alina. In my mind's eye Alina is in the photo too, holding my hand and laughing. I have imagined her with me in London so often it is as if she has always been here. I listen to the trains and picture her on one travelling to meet me. I will be at the barrier, and straightaway we will find our own corner and dance and time will not exist. I open my eyes and my vision is blurred. I message Alina, and when there is no reply, I ring her. She doesn't pick up. I watch the station clock, the gold hand shuddering from one minute to the next. I am not ready to move. Something is wrong; my head is spinning and my heart is aching. It has been fierce behind my ribs for days. I cup my palm over it, and it is there and real, ticking fast and large.

A message pings in and my heart trips, but it is not Alina. It is Phoebe. Haha, she says, my card was under the chair by the door. Sorry if I worried you. See you Monday?

I breathe into our hearts, Alina's and mine, bring fresh air to bend the pain, fill them with so much air I worry that it will leak out through the cracks.

Via del Tramvai
Han Smith

Venusbassin

It was the summer of our maturity, or at least of our maturità:
the exams that marked the end of our schooling and would
determine the rest of our lives, perhaps. Once they were over,
we had a week to fill before the results would be taped to
the double door of the school, and it was during that week
that Mauro decided we should visit, together, one last time,
each of the three villas that our province was mildly famous
for. The villa with the ruins was within walking distance and
the villa with the fountains and the one with the waterfalls
we caught the blue bus into town to reach. We would take
the perfect photograph of ourselves, with something iconic
behind us, at each. I was surprised by Mauro's suggestion
at first, though not by anyone else's quick acceptance of it,
and the prospect of the visits among the slow movements of
American and German tourists was something that appealed
to me. We meant absolutely nothing to them. At the same
time our mission would be the answer, it already seemed, to
a question I had not yet quite allowed myself to ask. It was a
question about the cloud or other quality of air that had hung
between us for the past year, or more, and about what might

169

arise to take its place. It was about what, if anything, would continue to exist: between us as one group and in smaller configurations, and between the individuals we were shaped or shaping into.

Devil's Appendix

On the day that we started with the villa with the ruins, I arrived before the others outside Claudio's building. I stood next to the containers for glass and metal cans and felt the heat the green plastic was pulsing without touching it. It was the middle of the morning and it was difficult to remember when my skin had last been under the sun for so long.

Claudio emerged from the door with a large backpack. Cheese and bread, he said. And cherries. Just to make it a proper outing.

His pale shirt was the collared kind he had started wearing some months before, and the sleeves were folded to his elbows, and he wore trousers. What about matching caps, I said. Or a flag to make sure no one gets left behind.

Left behind is just bad luck, he said.

Gabriele appeared, and then Marilena, carrying the retracted poles of a camera stand.

He's already asked if it's a gun and it's not, she said.

Mauro and Elisa were last. They came into view together and Marilena raised her eyebrows, her head still facing us and not them. Interesting, she said. Very interesting.

We went to buy water, said Elisa when they had reached us. She pointed to the bag that Mauro was holding. I saw that her thumbnails were painted silver. The nails, bitten tight, of her fingers were not.

I took one of the bottles as Mauro passed them around. He

took back Elisa's once she had opened it and taken three sips, and placed it into the bag again with his. I saw that Marilena noticed this, too.

Come on, said Claudio. Before all the coaches get there.

Vedovelle

We hadn't beaten the coaches by any means, but the last of a large group had just trailed in after their guide so there was no queue when we entered the ticket booth. A friend of Gabriele's cousin's was at the counter. Come for some culture? she said when she saw us. Shouldn't you be at the sea, or something?

Mauro lifted a leaflet from the shelf and tapped at an image on the front of it earnestly. The emperor? Really? he said. He really lived here? We don't even have emperors in California anymore!

Claudio pulled the leaflet from him and swiped it at Mauro's arm. He frowned in consideration at the image himself. This could be good, for our photo, he said.

Marilena glanced at it too, and touched it. I think I fell in that canal part, once, she said. When my parents' friends from the north were visiting. I cried and we had to go home, I think.

And there's a crocodile there, or something, said Elisa. Isn't there a statue of a crocodile?

I remembered at that moment that there was a marble crocodile, and that I had once been convinced, on a visit with relatives, that I had seen its tail twitch. My mother had assured me that it must have been the light, but my father had crouched with me and whispered: Maybe it only comes alive for special souls. Maybe this is a secret to keep.

I remembered this but I was also thinking of the stories I

had used to invent, in whispers, with Elisa, and the things we had made her brother believe. I was thinking of all of this in one instant, and also picturing the classroom at school, where Elisa had sat next to me for geography and literature: a room I would probably never sit in again.

Turta di Spus

Time towed as thickly and strangely as I had half expected it would as we drifted between the stone and clay remnants. Gabriele and Mauro posed on the broken plinths and Marilena used the leaflet to score a fan. We ate the bread and strips of cheese beneath two trees, with Claudio's backpack against a jagged column, and made a circle of the cherry stones on top. Gabriele kicked them off before we left.

When the sun was at its highest, we went into the museum hut, where it was dark and cool and a line of white-haired women were sitting on the benches by the door, looking bored. Claudio said we should pay attention to the mosaics, and when Marilena said they were just pieces of smashed rock, he said that they were not rocks but ceramics, glass and marble. There was one of doves perched tightly around a bronze bowl, the beak of one bird piercing the water's surface and white fragments showing the ripple and reflections. The other doves' heads were turned away from the bowl. I read on a label of text that it was said that real birds had been confused by the mosaic and had often tried to land on the rim, and been injured.

Outside again, at a pool surrounded by statues, I thought of making a joke about real humans attempting to join their naked, still bodies. I wondered if Elisa was looking for the crocodile. I wondered what she felt across her shoulders whenever Mauro's arm rested around them, for longer and longer each time. I tried to pace my legs to keep a rhythm with each of the others, in turn.

Soča/Isonzo

Marilena spotted the two men first, or in any case, she was the first to point them out.

By the signpost, she said. Seriously? Out here?

Further back in the direction we had come from before leaning on the low walls of what had been the baths, the men were walking hand in hand, and towards us. One was saying something to the other, quietly so that the second tipped his head. He nodded, and laughed, and the two of them stopped briefly. The first touched the second man's hip at the belt.

God, said Marilena. And that ring on his thumb.

I willed them to walk further apart. To stop again and turn back to the museum rooms. To remember that they were supposed to be waiting, and to greet two women, finally catching up, with a kiss each or at least an embrace.

The men came closer, still ducking at each other.

Watch, said Mauro. Just watch this. Gabriele?

Gabriele creased his eyes at Mauro, next to him, and flickered with both an eagerness and apprehension. Mauro tilted towards him and slid one arm around his waist. Gabriele flinched. Just play it, said Mauro.

The only sound was the men's steps on the grit.

Hi there, said Mauro, in English, squinting up as they levelled with us. He raised the hand that was not pressed against Gabriele. You like this place? It's beautiful here, no?

The bearded, shorter man smiled at Mauro, and Gabriele, scanned the rest of us quickly along the row, and then returned his gaze to Mauro. Yes, he said. It's unbelievable, just gorgeous. You're from here or just visiting too?

We're from here, said Mauro. Or, I am from here, and Ricky – this is Ricky – he is from the city. He comes here only tonight and I want to show him something very special, so I bring him here.

Gabriele drew his lips into a smile and dropped his eyes to the rubber on his shoes.

Special my arse, said Mauro in dialect. He sounded precisely like his father, and his uncle. Special is what these whores show each other, he said.

The bearded man and the taller man exchanged glances.

He doesn't speak English, said Mauro. I translate for him.

I wouldn't need English to crush their filthy faces in, said Gabriele.

He says he hopes you like it here, said Mauro. He says he hopes you have no troubles here, you know.

The tense parts of the taller man's face seemed to loosen. Thank you, he said. That's so sweet.

The bearded man pushed his tongue between his teeth and gestured to the paths that led back to the entrance. Definitely not welcome everywhere, though, he said. I thought the woman with the tickets was almost about to spit on us, or something.

Respect to your cousin and her friend, then, Mauro said, and Gabriele cursed and repeated the same, and added: Trying to save us. If only.

He says are you staying in the city or out here? said Mauro.

We're actually pretty close to here, said the bearded man. He named the neighbouring town, where the school and other two villas were. But we've been going to the city in the evenings more, to go out, he said.

Thank the lord for that, said Gabriele.

Yes, that's the more safe idea, said Mauro.

So why are they still here? Enough, said Gabriele. Come on, before I actually vomit.

Mauro beamed at the two of them, waiting, and stretched his neck. So really, have a wonderful time here, he said. I'm serious. We really hope you enjoy it. I tell you, you look fantastic together.

The bearded man showed no recognition that Mauro was imitating his own voice and rhythms. It was the taller man who had narrowed his eyes. He said something in German to the bearded one, softly, and then said to Mauro: OK, nice to talk with you.

OK, said Mauro. Enjoy this beautiful day. This gorgeous day. You really deserve that.

As the men moved on, beneath one of the arches, walking without touching and not appearing to be speaking, either, Gabriele continued to curse, and Marilena said that the pair of them should be on television, and were classics. Let's wait for those results next week and I'll consider it, said Mauro.

I stood and brushed flakes from my palms and thighs. I had ground a small slate from the wall into sharp pieces.

Are we taking that photograph or what? said Claudio.

Navigli

Eventually, we took the picture back at the square pool. Mauro stood behind a statue without a head so that the marble formed his torso and limbs, and we took one with him in this position and the rest with all of us in a line along the water. Each time Gabriele pressed the button and ran to join us in the seconds before the click, he pretended to hurtle over the edge. Just fall in and get it over with, said Elisa.

We didn't find the crocodile, and so I couldn't show it to her. She stood between Mauro and Marilena for the photographs, and I was on the end, next to Claudio, like I had been for physics and religion, by the window blinds.

Eisbachwelle

At seven, when the villa closed, Gabriele suggested going to his brother's bar, but Elisa said she wanted to shower and Claudio said his uncle was expected for dinner. Instead we stopped at the park that was at the junction of the road to the villa. It was the park we had often come to as children. There was a larger one now, with spiral slides, near the shopping centre, and this one was empty as we walked across it.

It's clearly some kind of sign, said Marilena. Something about our lost youth, or whatever.

We passed through to the lane at the far end of the park, where Gabriele and some other boys had built a base in the bushes one summer. The lane had a name: Via del Tramvai, but the tram tracks were fully overgrown and for cars it was a pointless dead end.

It was no girls allowed, said Gabriele. We were making secret weapons. The glory days.

Weapons out of mud, said Mauro.

Gabriele pointed. It must have been here, he said.

It's a ditch, said Claudio.

Gabriele turned to me. Fede, he said. You tried attacking us, remember?

I just thought it was idiotic that you wouldn't let us in, I said. I remembered his dirt-wiped face, and the older boys.

Like you wanted to start a revolution, he said. Didn't you come with water guns, one time?

Elisa tugged one dry strand of the long grass. If you recall, she said, you fought back with brick pieces. Six or seven of you against two girls.

At least you're a reformed man now, said Claudio.

Gabriele made a peace sign with his fingers. Of course, he said.

San Francesco Che Parla agli Uccelli

When I unlocked the door to our apartment, my parents were watching television with the lights off. The colours from the screen printed shapes across their faces and I could see that the film was coming to an end.

How was the villa? my father asked. He remembered, always, everything I said to him but hadn't looked away from the glow. I was thinking about the lot of you, before you all fly away and then who knows, he said.

It was nice, I said. We took a photograph together. We're doing one for each of the villas.

Come and watch this last bit with us, my mother said. She moved a cushion with the side of her arm.

I sat on the extended part of the sofa and crossed my legs at the ankles. I closed my eyes. I thought of the taller man's changing expression, and the quick glint of silver thumbnails in the sun. I wondered why it was that when my parents were so good to me, through no fault of their own I could tell them almost nothing.

Morske Orgulje

The next morning, Marilena phoned to say she was working with her mother for the day, and we would go to the villa with the fountains the day after. My parents had both already left and I sat at the table for nearly two hours, reading every page of the newspaper. At midday I went to the third floor and asked our neighbour if she wanted me to pick up her two children, who I had sometimes looked after the summer before. I collected them and took them to the new park. When I asked if they ever went to the old one, they looked blank.

Pistyll Rhaeadr

When we left the bus at the square in the town and did not cross automatically to the school, what I felt was more like weightlessness than freedom. That'll be where they execute me, for failing, said Claudio, gesturing to the steps. Claudio would easily be within the top three marks. He said things like this with his eyes pinched shut, his hand poised like a pistol at his temple.

Ago, Filo, Nodo

In the painted rooms of the villa itself, we lingered only at the most dramatic hunting scenes, and at a bloated angel that Gabriele insisted was identical to our biology teacher. We came out into the sunlight on the terrace.

Mauro thrust his elbows over the balustrade, with his back to it, and levered himself to sit on it in one movement. Get up here, he said, and Gabriele looked up, but it was Elisa he was speaking to.

Joss Bay

Marilena gave her verdict on each of the fountains and decided if they suited for the photograph. The grotto with the shells was aesthetically perfect, she said, but smelled too much of real sea.

We reached the slope of the Cento Fontane, where water spouted from one hundred mouths of monkeys, bears and other carved animals. Gabriele bent over the channel that the jets ran into and scooped a handful that he brought to his own mouth. He turned, aligned himself with the stone faces on either side, and a stream slushed out from between his lips.

One hundred and one fountains now, he said. He wiped his chin and exaggerated a bow.

You're insane, said Claudio.

But still, said Mauro. What about this? I'm not going to put that scum near my mouth, but what if we used bottled water? We could all line up and take the picture here.

Wattenmeer

Marilena, as soon as the three of them had left to buy more water at the café at the top, sat down next to Elisa and said: So you and Mauro? Do you at least want to tell us if it's going to be after the results or before?

Who says it has to be anything, said Elisa.

Adige

The faces I stooped between for the photograph were a lion and a less realistic creature with horns and eyes that were bulged and wild. I took the new bottle from Elisa and poured the liquid into my mouth. I touched my bottom lip to the plastic while pretending that I was trying not to, like the others.

179

This is what that external examiner needs to see, said Mauro when we had managed a version with everybody spilling the torrent at the same time. That's us puking all over her stupid questions.

I tried to make the water taste sweet as I held it, even though it strained my tongue.

Avery Hill Conduit Head

We were on the slope back to the terrace, uphill. It was late and hardly anyone was still coming down. And then someone was just ahead, approaching. Mauro, at the front with Gabriele, turned around with his jaw mock-dropped. Look who's back for more, he said.

The bearded man and the taller man, in step but with a gap between them, appeared to recognise Gabriele first. The bearded man opened his mouth and began to raise his outside arm, and in the same moment Gabriele looked to Mauro, who was glaring directly ahead, beyond the men. Narrowly missing the bearded man's sleeve, he moved straight past them without a glance. Gabriele then did exactly the same.

Marilena brushed past, then Elisa, and me, and Claudio, and all in silence.

Excellent, said Mauro. That was priceless. To Gabriele he said: Turn around. Are they looking?

Gabriele turned briefly. Yes, he said. Or wait. I mean –

What? said Marilena. This is bizarre now. Maybe, we could just have – we could have –

They're looking at Claudio, said Gabriele. Not now, but they were. It was definitely Claudio.

We reached the flat surface of the terrace, and Mauro halted. He studied Claudio. I thought so too, he said.

What? said Claudio. They were looking at all of us.

I don't know, said Mauro. They should have been looking at me, and Gabriele.

They were, said Claudio. Of course they were.

But they were looking at you like they knew you, said Mauro.

Claudio breathed out through his nostrils. That doesn't even make sense, he said.

Why would they recognise you? said Mauro.

All of us were there the other day, said Elisa. They remembered all of us from then. They must have.

You didn't speak to them the other day, said Mauro. Why would they look at you like that?

Like what? They were looking at all of us, said Elisa. I told you. I saw them. And why wouldn't they look? With a picture of youth like us, can you blame them?

And Claudio's the most tempting of all, said Mauro. Apparently. Or what?

That's obvious, said Claudio. His hand swiped fluidly down his jeans.

I still think it's strange, said Gabriele.

You can't blame them for having good taste, said Claudio. His voice was louder again and we had almost arrived at the end of the tiles. He nodded, the smallest nod, to Elisa, as we crossed the threshold back into the villa, where a woman in padded shoes was switching off the lights. The corners of the dark rooms were beckoning caverns.

Куру-Узень

We were in the long grass at Via del Tramvai again. We had headed to the bar from the bus stop on the main road, and

Gabriele had waved to someone inside, and then we had passed it already, and kept on. With our feet above the ditch, Marilena said we should think about what to do after the results. To celebrate, she said. We should go to the sea, or something.

Mauro said we would need a car, and then was quiet. Claudio said he would be staying with his grandparents and working on their allotment in the mountains all summer.

No one believes that, Gabriele said. We all know you've got someone up there.

Maybe, said Claudio. Maybe not.

Mauro said something about coarse girls from the mountains and Claudio's relief was in his shrug.

Chiostro delle Rane

In my room, after eating with my parents, I slid the diary I had bought in September from the stack of books at the bottom of my wardrobe. It had a ridged and ugly, coated cover and I had filled it in every day for three weeks. I could hear the voices of others in what I'd written, overlaid on or dissolved in my own. I'm never going to pass history, I read, because Montesani only likes the tall girls. Marilena's sister is pregnant and dead meat. I like the book we started today but I don't know how to put it in good words. Elisa came with me to the library in the break and she drew a polar bear cub on my folder.

Then: Elisa writes summaries that sound like real essays and she doesn't even realise it. Elisa doesn't smoke anymore. The only person who understood the poem we read about salt echoes was Elisa. Elisa remembers the time I broke the lamp in the middle-school music room and cried, still.

I'd stopped writing in the diary because I had too much to do in the evenings, and also because the left-hand pages were awkward, and also because it made things too solid.

Skradinski Buk

While the blue bus climbed the hill to the town again, I tried to recall the waterfalls from memory. They would be cooling and purifying, and a person could perhaps glide into one, cascade away with it. Sitting next to Claudio, I felt suddenly, though I'd always known, that he would soon be distant, and that I would miss him. I wanted to know that his face would be as calm and clear, somewhere, as it was when he described the ripe tomatoes he ate with his grandmother.

Halliste

What I remember about the villa with the waterfalls is this:

The steep, downward paths. The temple remains jutting over the rock, where Mauro this time produced not water but wine, and plastic cups and napkins from his bag. Elisa and Marilena on the ledge between two pillars; Mauro pretending to be a real photographer. More attitude, he said. That's it. The river-eroded caves out of reach. The group picture, afterwards, in front of the great fall, all leaping into the air, suspended. Clipping back the stand and beginning the long ascent. A plummeting, already drained sensation.

Roški Slap

What I remember about the villa with the waterfalls is this:

Close to the top, damp with sweat through our shirts, and Elisa stopped in the middle of the path. I'm an idiot, she said. My keys are down there.

Your keys? said Marilena. What do you mean?

My keys, said Elisa. I took them out because they dug into my leg when we were jumping for the photo. I put them down.

This happened: I could see where the keys were. I knew.

I'll go, said Mauro.

Marilena mouthed: Of course.

I don't mind, said Mauro. These muscles aren't just made for looking at, after all.

Wait, I said. I know where they are.

Befreiung-der-Quelle

I turned and walked. I remembered the gleaming. Surely I did. I was walking alone, towards the metal flash.

And then I was no longer walking alone. There were steps behind me, faster than mine, and I would not look round because they might still disappear.

I'm coming, said Elisa. She was behind me, then beside me.

Styggforsen

What do you think you'll remember? she said.

We both looked ahead, towards the next bright or shaded patch. Remember? I said. About this week?

This? she said. No. I mean this year, or everything.

You mean our precious education, I said. Our formation.

Probably we'll remember things that we don't quite even notice now, she said.

We walked on. I tried to think of something that was right to say.

We've hardly spoken since the exams began, she said.

We've had these three days, I said.

It's different, she said. It's not the same, is it?

We rounded another curve and I thought of something. It was something one of the writers we'd studied had said in a book about her family and their language. I'd know them in the darkest cave, I said.

That's good, she said. I like that one, too.

Écluse de l'Aiguille

Mauro's borrowing a car, she said. We're going to the sea. He's booked a room.

I know where the keys are, I said. I saw them.

He's booked a room with a balcony and two sunchairs on the beach, she said.

You put them down where you were tying your laces, I said.

He's serious, she said. And I am. I have to be. I'm not going to study and go anywhere like you are. This is the only way I can be.

You can study, I said. Of course you can.

He's serious, she said. He's a good person, or he will be. He shows off but he's a good person and he cares.

You can study, I said. You can go where you want to go.

Basiliskenbrunnen

I knelt and I picked up the keys. They were dusty, reflecting nothing now, and were all I had to give to her.

I know what he did yesterday with those men was wrong, she said. And the first day. He was only joking. It's just something his father would do and he was just performing, she said.

I held out the keys on the knotted ribbon.

I'll tell you something, she said. Claudio told me to leave them here and make you see. He knew you'd see and he knew you'd come back down for me.

Claudio, I said.

Claudio, she said. He went to the city the other night, late, to the bar for the men that – to the bar for men. He saw those two from the villa there. They saw him.

Claudio's getting away, I said.

Yes, she said.

Дружба Народов

I stared into the great fall and thought of all the dashing water I could that never stopped. I saw falling rain, cracking waves, the fountains, ripples, river bends, and trickled flames. I thought of a noise that would fill me and leave no space.

Fede, she said. Don't do that. Don't cry.

I stepped nearer to the fall. It's loud enough, I said.

She came closer too, and closer to me.

Touch the water, I said. Put your whole head inside.

Fede, she said.

Like this, I said.

Križna Jama

Her face was a feeling next to my face. Her mouth touched my cheek before my own lips, and she bit hard and then was only warm, and just once.

I can't, she said, and the waterfall sank her words.

Fede, she said.

In another life, she said.

It's not who we are, she said. It's where we are. And who they are.

The great fall battered our skin almost numb.

Vogeltränkebrunnen

On the path she held my hand until the last, monstrous corner. She slipped it free, and there were the others.

Why are you drenched? said Marilena. What happened?

It was hot, said Elisa. The only way to cool down.

Before we had reached the bus stop, we were dry.

Sgwd Einion Gam

At Via del Tramvai, that night, we sat once again above the ditch, and then lay back. Claudio named constellations and said that light pollution was a disgrace to us all. The sky I saw was stark and parched. Even the moon was simply bare. I wrote a wish for Claudio to read between the stars.

And this I knew I would hold as my image, even when we had printed the photographs and bought six sets of gold, garish frames. I would stand them on the desk in the tired city I would shiver in, in the years to come. But every time I sought out fleeting water for its surge and dance, there in that city and, later, elsewhere, this was the composition I always summoned: lying less than a head away from Elisa, and from all the others, with the useless tram tracks invisible under everything, but there.

Contributors' Bios

Lucy Sweeney Byrne's work has appeared in *Banshee*, *The Stinging Fly*, *The Dublin Review*, *3:AM*, *Litro* and *Grist*, with further work forthcoming in *gorse*. Her story collection, *Paris Syndrome*, was published by Banshee Press in 2019. In 2020, Lucy was longlisted for the Edge Hill Short Story Prize and shortlisted for the Kate O'Brien Award, John McGahern Annual Book Prize, Butler Literary Award and Dalkey Emerging Writer Award.

Although **Rea Dennhardt** has always written, it's mostly been around jobs that were not about writing at all. Her CV is broad: papergirl, barmaid, barista; finance, football, fashion, start-ups. After twenty years overseas, she is now based in London, doing an MA in creative writing and working for a charity getting young people into entrepreneurship. Twitter: @readennhardt

Kevin Dyer. Writer, theatre director, dramaturg. He won the Writers' Guild of Great Britain (WGGB) Award for Best Play for Young Audiences for *The Monster Under the Bed*; is published by Aurora; and was awarded the Inspirational Playwrights Award at the International Association of Theatre for Children and Young People (ASSITEJ) World Congress in Cape Town. His first novel, *Marion*, is about a cow. www.kevindyer.co.uk

Kate Ellis is a writer and bookseller based in London. Her short fiction has been published in the *Open Pen Anthology*, *The Mechanics' Institute Review* and *The London Short Story Prize Anthology* among others. In 2020, she was longlisted for the Deborah Rogers Foundation Award for her debut novel. She runs the Brick Lane Bookshop Short Story Prize. @katesmalleyelli

Alice Haworth-Booth is a short-story writer. Her work won the 2019 Aurora Prize for short fiction and was shortlisted for the 2020 Nobrow Short Story Competition. With her sister Emily, she is currently writing an illustrated history of protest for children, to be published in spring 2021.

Jack Houston is a writer from London and is poet-in-residence at Hackney Libraries. His poetry has featured in *Poetry London*, *The Rialto* and *Stand*, and been commended in the UEA's sex-writing symposium I'll Show You Mine Prize. His short fiction was shortlisted for the BBC National Short Story Award 2020.

K. Lockwood Jefford is originally from Cardiff and now lives in Folkestone. She has worked in NHS mental health services and has an MA in creative writing from Birkbeck. She won the H. G. Wells Short Story Prize and the Sunderland-Waterstones (Sun) Short Story Award, and was highly commended in the TLC Pen Factor Prize. Her work appears in several print anthologies and MIROnline. She is working on a collection of short fiction and a novel.

Cllr Dr **Denise Jones**, HonDLitt, FRSA, Freeman of the City of London, studied graphic design, was a primary school teacher and has worked with the bookshop that she co-founded since 1978. She lives in Cable Street and is an elected Labour councillor in Tower Hamlets. Denise strongly supports the arts and is a board member of Rich Mix, the V&A Museum of Childhood, Trinity Buoy Wharf Trust, Create London, Aldgate & Allhallows Foundation, Mulberry Academy Trust and Lee Valley Regional Park Authority.

Huma Qureshi was a journalist before she started writing short stories, but short stories are where her heart lies. This year, she won the 2020 *Harper's Bazaar* Short Story Prize and last year, she placed second in the 2019 Benedict Kiely Short Story Competition. Her collection of short stories, *Things We Do Not Tell The People We Love*, was shortlisted for the SI Leeds Literary Prize, 2020. Her memoir, *How We Met*, will be published in January 2021 by Elliott & Thompson. She is now writing her first novel.

Gemma Reeves is a writer and teacher from London. She has been shortlisted for the V. S. Pritchett Short Story Prize and highly commended in the Bridport Short Story Prize. *Victoria Park*, Gemma's debut novel, will be published by Atlantic Books in January 2021, and simultaneously in audio by Bolinda.

Han Smith is a queer writer, translator and adult literacy teacher, and has been shortlisted/longlisted for the *Mslexia* Novella Competition, the Desperate Literature Prize and the UEA New Forms Award. Also published and commissioned by *Versopolis*, *Hotel*, *Litro*, Liars' League and the European Poetry Festival, Han received a London Writers Award in 2019 and has one novel currently on submission and another in progress. Twitter: @Han_Smiff; web: www.han--smith.com

Kieran Toms grew up in Ilford, east London, and lives in Peckham, south-east London. He is inspired to write by what he likes to read: fiction, non-fiction, fragments from the internet, handwritten notes found on the street. He is in an excellent book club, which was formed by strangers at a nightclub.

Rajasree Variyar is an Indian-Australian now based in London. She's currently completing her master's in creative writing at the University of East Anglia. Her short story 'Lucky Buddha' was runner-up in the 2019 *Shooter* Short Story Competition, and her novel-in-progress, *The Wanted Girl*, was shortlisted for the 2019 Mo Siewcharran Prize for unpublished novels.

Andrea Watts is a writer from Hackney. Her stories have been published in anthologies and placed in competitions. She has a fine art degree from Chelsea and a master's in creative and life writing from Goldsmiths, where she was shortlisted for the Pat Kavanagh Prize.

Judges' Quotes

1ˢᵗ Prize
The Closed Door – Alice Haworth-Booth

'*The Closed Door* has a wry, energetic voice that is very compellingly crafted; its project – both intimate and political – is stylishly alert to the contemporary, and I loved its candour and wit: "It was shockingly easy to make a life."'

Harriet Moore

'*The Closed Door* is a joyful and constantly surprising story, with an energy and wit reminiscent of Grace Paley.'

Chris Power

'I enjoyed the political element in this original, well-crafted story. It feels totally topical, and I found its attitude inspiring.'

Sharmaine Lovegrove

2nd Prize

To Those Born Later – Kieran Toms

'A vivid, moving, atmospheric story which has its own dark poetry – a white minibus in the dark; "a few houses, lonely sentinels in the nothingness"; men drowning in brackish hinterland. I loved its formally graceful use of the speculative – authorities spraying green curfew dust, family deaths "in the sicknesses"; it had a fresh, inventive strangeness.'

Harriet Moore

3rd Prize

Fix – K. Lockwood Jefford

'This story was distinguished formally in how it explores, in an exacting style and smart structure, the complex ways our lives intersect with others.'

Harriet Moore

'Tight and tense, *Fix* provokes an emotional response without ever breaking its own rule of cold, forensic remove.'

Chris Power

Shortlisted Stories

Chameleon – Rea Dennhardt

'This story was full of vitality and tactility; it had its own distinctive imagery and vernacular – tea roses, "a dead, blue kitten", "Do pink cats behave pinker?", blond Domestos, "chicken-mushroom-cloud pie", "I told him I was goose liver". The narrating voice had a vibrant interior life – intricate and alert to the emotional truths of grief and childhood.'

Harriet Moore

No Phones at the Dinner Table – Jack Houston

'There was a wonderful immediacy to the style of this story; it was emotionally vivid with an attentiveness to eloquent, small details.'

Harriet Moore

'I admire the way this story's stream of consciousness narration vividly realises its pre-teenage narrator's situation, as she navigates the rituals and fractures of family life.'

Chris Power

Small Differences – Huma Qureshi

'Strong.'

Sharmaine Lovegrove

'A tonally and emotionally sophisticated story which portrayed – with polish and precision – familial dynamics, and how hard it can be to breach them; how you can be made to feel excluded by the "vanity of small differences" – even in love.'

Harriet Moore

Longlisted Stories

Night Classes – Lucy Sweeney Byrne

'An accomplished story interestingly engaged with the possibilities of freedom.'

Harriet Moore

The Bread Man – Kevin Dyer

'A moving, understated story with a good sense of authorial control.'

Harriet Moore

Sharing Time – Gemma Reeves

'I liked this very much, an affecting story. Shows the serendipity of lives intersecting.'

Sharmaine Lovegrove

Via del Tramvai – Han Smith

'A poised and artful story with a central, tense set piece exploring homophobia which is elegantly and powerfully articulated.'

Harriet Moore

The Bhootham in the Mango Tree – Rajasree Variyar

'A richly detailed story full of excellent, poetic imagery and sentences.'

Harriet Moore

Spiders – Andrea Watts

'Loved this.'

Sharmaine Lovegrove

'A smart portrayal of power dynamics and privilege with some beautiful accompanying descriptive details.'

Harriet Moore

Longlist

'This collection holds such an illuminating and vivid range of stories from an exciting array of new voices already so accomplished in their craft.'

Sharmaine Lovegrove

'An impressive collection of stories full of verve, emotional enquiry and imagination. From atmospheric settings and distinctive images to stylish precision and exactitude, the multiple and intricate ways of seeing, feeling and thinking that can be found in these stories are invigorating.'

Harriet Moore

'I really appreciate the range and ambition on display in these stories. These are writers putting work into voice and craft rather than relying on event alone, and that's what makes their work persist in the mind.'

Chris Power

Thanks

Every writer who entered this year's competition.

The twelve longlisted writers whose excellent stories make up this anthology.

First readers: Andrew Carson, Glenn Collins, Kalina Dimitrova, Jane Earl, Chris Ellis, Andrew Everitt, Harry Gallon, Olivia Griffiths, Alison Hitchcock, Elinor Johns, Joe Johnson, Denise Jones, Jarred McGinnis, Roger Mills, Pema Monaghan, Sophia Pearson, Tamara Pollock, Sean Preston, Veena Sharma and Adelaide Turnbull.

Second readers: Xanthi Barker and Max Sydney Smith.

Judges: Sharmaine Lovegrove, Harriet Moore and Chris Power.

Polly Jones for anonymising.

Kalina Dimitrova for finance.

Denise Jones for her foreword.

All at Brick Lane Bookshop for believing in the competition and for their support.

Sue Tyley, our invaluable copy-editor.

Peter J. Coles, Christina Carè and last year's winner James Mitchell for making time to record a podcast – twice!

Our stockists: Pages of Hackney, Burley Fisher Books, Libreria, Riverside Bookshop, No Alibis Bookstore, Rough Trade, Snap, Daunt Books and Broadway Bookshop.

Everyone who bought and read the 2019 anthology.

Friends and supporters on- and offline, including last year's longlistees, *Open Pen*, Spread the Word, Comma Press, Republic of Consciousness Prize, MIROnline, Influx Press, *Sunday Times* Audible, and many others.

Online listings: writers-online.co.uk, nawe.co.uk, mironline.org, duotrope.com, neonbooks.org.uk, aerogrammestudio.com, christopherfielden.com, pocketmags.com, shortstoryaward.co.uk and nothingintherulebook.com.

Goodreads reviewers.

Clays printers.

Brick Lane Bookshop customers.

My favourite people for being excited about and supportive of the project all over again.